Wyoming Refuge

Wyoming Refuge

A Havoc in Wyoming Prequel

Millie Copper

Copyright © 2019 CU Publishing LLC
ISBN-13: 978-1-7327482-6-2

Written by Millie Copper
Edited by Ameryn Tucker
Proofread by Light Hand Proofreading

Also by Millie Copper

Havoc in Wyoming Series

Havoc in Wyoming: Part 1, Caldwell's Homestead

Havoc in Wyoming: Part 2, Katie's Journey

Havoc in Wyoming: Part 3, Mollie's Quest

Havoc Begins: A Havoc in Wyoming Story (Part 3.5)

Havoc in Wyoming: Part 4, Shields and Ramparts

Havoc in Wyoming: Part 5, Fowler's Snare

Havoc Rises: A Havoc in Wyoming Story (Part 5.5)

Havoc in Wyoming: Part 6, Pestilence in the Darkness

Christmas on the Mountain: A Havoc in Wyoming Novella

Havoc Peaks: A Havoc in Wyoming Story (Part 6.5)

Havoc in Wyoming: Part 7, My Refuge and Fortress

Montana Mayhem Series

Unending Havoc: Montana Mayhem Book 1

Ruthless Havoc: Montana Mayhem Book 2

Merciless Havoc: Montana Mayhem Book 3

Nonfiction Books

Stock the Real Food Pantry: A Handbook for Making the Most of Your Pantry

Design a Dish: Save Your Food Dollars

Real Food Hits the Road: Budget Friendly Tips, Ideas, and Recipes for Enjoying Real Food Away from Home

Stretchy Beans: Nutritious, Economical Meals the Easy Way

Join My Reader's Club!

As part of my reader's club, you'll be the first to know about new releases and specials. I also share info on books I'm reading, preparedness tips, and more, please sign up on my website:

MillieCopper.com

Chapter 1

Sam Mitchell

"Sam, what's that noise?" She leans close, her breath tickling my ear.

I sit up taller in my chair, thinking it might give me a sound advantage. My wife's hearing is substantially better than mine. Georgia says it's part of being a mom. Even with all the commotion in our twins' third-grade classroom, she could probably still hear a mouse running down the hallway . . . on the other side of the school.

Nothing. I give a shrug and look back toward the speaker. Career Day. Up front is a mom who runs a ferret rescue. The children crush forward to get a better look and a touch.

"That's right, children, be nice and gentle with your pets," the mom croons.

I'm the last parent to talk, following Ferret Mom. Any chance of regaining their attention? Nope, doubt it. Georgia was fortunate to go first. Now, a half dozen people have gone, each with a better performance than the previous. The one before this, a baker, brought everyone a cupcake. Maybe I should've brought tongue depressors. *Ha.* That would've gone over well.

"Sam," Georgia grabs my arm, "there it is again."

This time, I might have heard something. But what I thought I heard . . . no, that wouldn't make any sense.

This is Groyver, Wyoming—not Iraq.

And then, suddenly, it seems I may be back in Iraq.

"Sam! Gunfire?" Georgia screeches.

I hear a scream and a shot.

The ferret petting ends abruptly as everyone turns to stare.

"I'll check it out," I say, wishing a few of the other parents wouldn't have left as soon as their turn was up. That one guy;

I can't remember his name, but he's an incredibly burly guy with the Groyver Fire Department. And I know he ignored the no-guns sign out front. I saw his sidearm when he stood up to give his talk.

"No!" Mrs. Jenkins yells, charging toward the door. "We're to go on immediate lockdown. No one in or out."

"Ma'am, I understand you have your protocol, but I'm not going to be a sitting duck. Feel free to lock the door after I leave."

"Dr. Mitchell, if you leave this room, you will not be allowed back in until this is over."

"I'm good with that."

Georgia, suddenly by my side, says, "I'll help."

I shake my head. "Can you stay? Take care of our children . . . all of the children. Call 911."

Georgia squeezes my hand and nods.

"Go! Just go!" Mrs. Jenkins demands, phone in hand. Ferret Mom, standing behind the teacher, is already on her phone, frantically crying for help.

I quietly slip out the door, steady myself in the alcove, and pull my Glock 23 from my inside-the-waistband holster. Yeah, this is a Gun-Free Zone, but apparently I'm not the only one who didn't get the memo.

I take a quick glance in the window of the classroom. Georgia is unholstering her own Glock, moving toward Mrs. Jenkins's desk.

Smart, use the desk for concealment.

The concrete walls and tile floor amplify a scream and discharge. The time between shots indicates someone's using self-control. Have I made the smartest choice? Maybe I should stay with Georgia, stand our ground in Mrs. Jenkins's classroom, and make sure my own kids are safe.

The way my heart is pounding, it's hard to believe I was ever in the military. Sure, as a Navy physician, I wasn't in the thick of it, but I'm not completely clueless. Before deploying for Operation Iraqi Freedom, I had plenty of advanced training. My entire squadron trained at a Marine Corps Air

Station. The training included the Pistol Expert Marksmanship Program.

That's when I discovered a love of firearms.

This love has carried through to current times, even sharing it with my wife and children. Georgia, raised in rural Idaho, was no stranger to guns. Chloe and Willie, our eight-year-old twins, are already excellent shots. Target practice is becoming a family affair. We even have our own practice range set up on a piece of land we purchased outside Groyver.

The amount of time I've spent handling weapons isn't the issue. The idea that someone out there has their own weapon, and sounds like they know how to use it—that's the rub. No doubt, they'll be shooting at me once I'm in view.

I crouch, peering around the wall into the hallway.

There he is. I take in as much as I can, then pull back quickly. Stay hidden for now.

He's considerably shorter than my six foot, three inches, and much lighter than my two hundred pounds, but obviously in excellent condition based on the way his biceps bulge in his black, long-sleeved T-shirt. Dressed in black combat boots, tactical pants, a vest, and a watchman's cap, he's even smudged his face in black paint. On first glance, his weapon looks like an AR-15. A handgun is also at his hip. I take note of his stride—purposeful and determined, but not worried or hurried.

The vest . . . is it a tactical vest for extra magazines or a flak-style vest containing body armor? Best to assume it's body armor.

Head shot. I'll need a head shot.

Crouching even lower, I risk a second quick look. The guy is closer, only about fifteen feet from the alcove. He's stopped, turned partially away.

A scream and two quick shots, not fired by this guy—these shots were farther away, the next hallway over.

A second shooter. Not good.

"Lord, help me. Guide me through this. Help me keep my wife and children—the children in this school—safe."

With my petition for assistance barely finished, the word *silent* comes to mind.

Silent. Silently. Take this guy out silently.

Hand-to-hand combat was part of my military training—limited and many years ago. While I have both a punching bag and a speed bag in my basement gym, I'm not terribly adept at fighting. I mainly use them to work up a good sweat. I haven't kept up on the training, the martial arts, or putting the hurt on someone. Never thought I'd need it once I left the service. But I'm good on the speed bag, able to strike in a workable rhythm to provide an excellent cardiovascular workout. That might come in handy.

My pocketknife. It's sharp, very sharp. Scalpel sharp. The knife might give me an advantage. My biggest advantage is going to be surprise and knowing where the knife will do the most damage.

Holstering my Glock, I pull out my Gerber pocketknife, bringing it to the ready. It has a four-inch blade, which suddenly feels way too small compared to an AR. What's the saying? *Don't bring a knife to a gun fight.*

A mistake? Better to just shoot the guy in the head and be done with it. Then deal with the second guy in the same manner.

A shuffle and slight scrape. Too late. The guy is here. What an idiot I am for switching to the knife. A slight shadow.

Time to rock and roll.

Chapter 2

Georgia Mitchell

I'm crouched behind the teacher's desk. The desk won't stop bullets, but it'll provide concealment to keep me hidden. If the shooter makes it through the locked door, I'll have the advantage of surprise.

Mrs. Jenkins, Ferret Mom—what was her name? Kristy? Krissy?—and the children, well away from the door and huddled in the corner, are also at the ready. Mrs. Jenkins moved a couple of the desks in front of the door, a flimsy barricade. Each of the children have been given something to throw if the intruder gets in the room. Books, stapler, whatever the teacher could grab and hand out. She's also instructed them that if the shooter breaches the door, they're to scream and yell, running around while pitching their "weapons" at him.

Yeah, sounds like an amazing plan. At least Ferret Mom has a wicked looking pair of scissors and seems set to strike.

My son, Willie, after receiving a book and instructions of use, said, quite seriously, "I'd prefer a gun, if you have one." Mrs. Jenkins looked at him like he had two heads. I have little doubt a talk with the principal will be required once this crisis has passed.

Of course, since both Sam and I are armed in a Gun-Free Zone, we might have more than the principal to deal with.

Where is Sam? The slim vertical window in the door gave me a few glimpses of him earlier, but nothing lately.

A scream and a shot, then another shot. Not Sam. Not close enough and not a pistol.

Unlike Sam, I was raised around guns of all sorts. While happy to have my 9-millimeter Glock, I'd love a pump shotgun loaded with number one buck, my preferred weapon and ammo for home defense. Not to mention, the sound of the pump leaves no doubt a person means business.

My Glock 19 holds fifteen rounds plus one in the chamber. I'm intimately acquainted with it, having spent several hundred hours at the range, along with taking several specialty classes with various firearms instructors over the years.

When Sam was getting ready for his second deployment, he had firearms training and caught the shooting bug. He's been supportive in encouraging me in my own training. I've even gone on several women's warrior weekends for advanced training. Likewise, Sam's had his own advanced training classes—postmilitary.

Three years ago, when Sam retired from active duty, one of the reasons we decided to settle in Wyoming was the gun-friendly attitude. We heard jokes about Wyoming having more firearms than people. At least, we thought it was a joke until we actually moved here. Wyomingites like their guns.

One thing we should've researched further was whether the school district allowed their staff to be armed. A few years ago, the Wyoming legislature enacted a rule allowing each individual district to decide. This district tabled the discussion after not reaching a decision. Now, when every second counts, I wish the teachers and staff were armed . . . and not just with books and staple guns.

Glancing at Mrs. Jenkins cowered in the corner, not even bothering to keep herself together, I change my mind. Mrs. Jenkins wouldn't—shouldn't—be armed.

Please, Lord, let Sam be okay. Let everyone be okay.

Chapter 3

Sam

Back flat against the wall of the alcove, four-inch blade at the ready, I stop breathing. The guy is here, crossing in front of the alcove.

I step into him. His face has time to register surprise, as I shove the knife into his throat, then quickly pull it back. The spurt of blood from the carotid is instant. The guy reacts by dropping his AR and moving both hands to his neck to stanch the bleeding. The clatter of the rifle hitting the tile causes me to cringe.

Where's the other guy?

I slam my elbow into this guy's nose, causing a slight *oomph* to escape from his diaphragm. Stab again, this time lower, the femoral artery in the groin area. Unless he receives immediate medical care, the guy will be a goner in minutes. Death by exsanguination. Or really, death by Sam Mitchell, MD.

I'm supposed to respect human life, not take it.

I pull out my handkerchief, *dirty handkerchief,* and jam it in the guy's mouth, then pull him fully into the alcove. I wish I had something to tie the guy up with. Probably no need. He's losing blood fast.

Another shot, still in a different hallway but sounding closer. Is there a third guy? Or is the second one making his way toward us?

Why didn't this guy go for his sidearm? I wonder, while relieving him of it and setting it out of his reach. Maybe he was too concerned about his neck being sliced open to think about anything further.

Blood drips from my hand as I softly knock on the classroom window. I leave a red smear behind to coat the window.

Georgia peeks out behind the teacher's desk. She sees me. I motion her to the door. She starts and stops, turning slightly. Her mouth is moving, talking. Undoubtedly Mrs. Jenkins is telling her not to go to the door. Georgia, gesticulating, finally gives an exaggerated shrug. Irritation paints her face as she strides to the door.

There's a scraping noise as she moves something, then cracks the door a little. "You okay?" she whispers.

"I'm okay, he's not." I gesture to the body on the ground. "He's not alone. There's at least one more."

She makes a face, quickly recovers, and asks, "Should I work on him?"

"No. Keep your weapon on him, but don't touch him. It's too late to— "

"Okay, I'm stepping out. Mrs. Jenkins is freaking out about this door being open."

I quietly say, "Might as well stay inside. Just keep an eye through the window. He's not going anywhere."

"Where are you going?" she whispers.

"After the other guy. The blood is everywhere. If he turns the corner, he'll see it."

"Be safe," Georgia says.

"Take care of our children. Take care of yourself," I say. I want to kiss her, hold her, tell her how much I love her, how she's been the best part of my life. We met in college, University of Washington—U Dub—both of us in the medicine program. We started the same year but didn't really get to know each other until the summer before our fourth year while on the same clerkship.

I had already joined the Navy, deciding a few months earlier that was the best way for me to become a doctor without being in debt for the rest of my life. Plus, I loved the idea of being able to give something back, to serve my country.

Georgia had plenty of doubts about a career in medicine. It wasn't really something she ever wanted. She was doing it for her mom. Her mom dreamed of being a doctor. She, too, was accepted to U Dub but got pregnant with Georgia. Instead of going to school, she married Georgia's dad, Ralph, ten years older and twice divorced co-owner of a heavy equipment business. Her mom never got over the loss of her dream. She pushed Georgia to fulfill the dream for her.

Georgia ended up deciding to pursue a DC, doctor of chiropractic. It's been a good fit for our family, especially when I was active duty. The hours were much more manageable than if she was also an MD.

A new noise—not a shot. A door rattling? Maybe. Still in the other hallway.

Stepping carefully to avoid sliding in the pool of blood, I again squat and peer out the alcove. Clear. I pick up the carbine—dropped by the almost dead guy—check it, making sure it's at the ready. The extra firepower will be helpful. I shove his pistol into my belt, at the small of my back. Not a place I prefer to carry a handgun, but better than leaving it for someone else to pick up.

Staying against the wall, I creep toward the middle hallway. The layout of this school is odd. Two halls running north to south, and three halls intersecting at the bottom, middle, and top. Each classroom has a small alcove before the doorway. In the past, I thought the alcoves were dumb. Now, not so much. This school is scheduled for remodeling. Built out of concrete block in the seventies, it's way past its prime. Today, I'm thinking that's a good thing.

I'm at the middle hallway, where I think the last shot may have originated. Once again in a crouch, I take a quick look.

Dressed identical, similar build, maybe built a little larger than the other guy. He's bent over a body. An adult body.

Now's the time.

I take a knee and a deep breath—heart pounding, mouth dry. The guy's back is to me. Should I shoot him in the back? The Navy officer part of me feels this is wrong. But the man in me has little problem with it. This guy is shooting up a school—a school full of children. How many are already dead?

My quandary is solved. The guy straightens slightly and begins to turn. I fire two quick shots, catching him in the rib cage. Guess the flak jacket isn't bulletproof. He discharges his weapon, shooting into the concrete-block wall.

Please let the block have stopped the bullets.

I stop cold. The unmistakable sound of a pistol sliding into position breaks the silence, followed by a terse, "Drop your weapon." My stomach falls.

The third shooter.

Chapter 4

Georgia

Several shots ring out, still in a different hallway.

Sam.

Please, God, let Sam be okay.

Mrs. Jenkins cries out, "They're coming for us! Be ready, children!"

I do my best not to roll my eyes, as I say, "The shots are a decent distance away. We're still fine."

She huffs in response.

I've kept most of my body behind the concrete wall, watching through the window. Several minutes ago, the guy in the alcove slumped over and slid down. The amount of blood on the floor, on the wall, and on the guy is substantial. Sam was right, lethal wounds.

It's been many minutes since the last shots. Every fiber in my being wants to open the door, to go find Sam. Make sure he's okay.

Several of the children are crying, which is understandable. My daughter, Chloe, is patting her friend on the back. "We'll be okay. We should stop crying so we can be ready."

With a snort, Mrs. Jenkins says, "It's okay to cry, children. There's no shame in it."

My Willie says, "How about we save the crying for later? Then we can be ready to fight if we need to."

Yep, definitely getting called into the principal's office. Principal Kent Skinner is a good guy. The year we moved to Groyver, the twins were just starting kindergarten. We met the principal at registration.

A Wyoming native, educated at the University of Wyoming, he has taught at many schools throughout the state and has been principal of Groyver Elementary for five years. We've spent time with him and his wife socially on several occasions. We even purchased a piece of property outside of town from him. Someday, we plan to build a place and move there.

Right now, we have a nice house in town, an easy walk from the school and a slightly longer walk to the office. Sam and I both work at the same practice, along with another physician, a doctor of osteopathic medicine.

Jeff Ridgely was originally looking for another DO to practice with him. Sam, not only an MD but also military, didn't really fit the mold of what Jeff thought his practice should be. Our desire to live in Wyoming caused Sam to push Jeff to at least spend some time talking, to find out if they might be a good fit for partnering.

Sam had an ace in the hole—me.

Jeff's long-term plan included adding a chiropractor, acupuncturist, and others to provide a holistic experience. I'm a chiropractor and massage therapist, which fits nicely with Jeff's future plans. We were able to offer an almost two-for-one deal, allowing him to build the practice quicker and for less money than he thought. It's been working extremely well.

Watching out the window, I see a shift in the light. Someone has made a shadow.

"Shh," I hiss to the teacher.

"No," Mrs. Jenkins broadcasts. "If he's getting in, we're to make noise, cause confusion. Children, get ready to throw your weapons and to scatter."

"How about you just keep quiet and let me use my weapon?"

This woman is something else.

"Humph."

The shadow fully materializes.

Chapter 5

Sam

"Dr. Mitchell?" The voice quivers. "Is that you?"

"It is," I respond cautiously, not turning around . . . also not dropping my weapon as previously ordered. I keep it trained on the bad guy.

"Oh, Doctor. You're such a bloody mess. I almost didn't recognize you. Is he dead? Did you get him?"

I study him closely. Is he breathing? I don't think so. "Yeah, looks like it. If you still have that gun trained on me, I'd appreciate it if you'd focus on him instead."

"Oh, sorry. It's down."

I move forward, kicking the downed shooter's AR out of reach, then checking for a pulse. Yep. Dead. I suck as a doctor today. I check the person on the floor. She's also gone.

I slowly turn. The school secretary. I can't remember her name.

"I think there's another guy," she says quietly. "I saw two of them dressed in black."

"Yeah, I, um, found the other one." I gesture at the blood covering me.

A look of confusion, quickly erased by understanding. "Oh . . . I see."

"There were only two?" I ask.

"Yes, but . . . well, there's a third. He's already dead."

"You got him?"

"No, they . . . I . . . I was in the staff restroom when it all, you know, started—when I heard the first shot. I wanted to hide." She sighs. "But it just didn't seem right. If they were hurting my kids, I couldn't just hide. I crept out of the bathroom, stayed in the alcove, and hunkered down. I saw two men in black walking away. They were just turning the corner. I waited a few moments, then snuck out."

I nod for her to continue.

"Kent—Principal Skinner—was in the hall, on the floor. I went to him, but he was dead." She chokes up, takes a deep breath, then continues, "He keeps a gun on his ankle and another in his office. I took the ankle one, but then went for the larger one in his office. This one." She nods her head toward the pistol in her hand.

"The third shooter?" I prod.

"Oh, yes. After I had the pistol— " she takes a ragged breath " —I found him, younger than this one." She motions to the dead guy on the floor. "He was already dead, propped up against the wall around the corner from the office. Did you take care of him first?"

"Nope. Didn't see him. Just this guy and another. I, uh, left him over by Mrs. Jenkins's classroom. My wife is watching him." No reason to say she was watching him die. "Have you called for help?"

"I called, but they already knew. I told them I'm armed. They said to stand down, but . . . "

"Hey," a loud whisper says. "Is he down?"

"Yes," the secretary says in a normal tone.

"I saw the kid by the office. Good job." A fit man in athletic shorts gives me a thumbs up. The gym teacher. I can't remember his name either, though we've met a few times. He even asked me to join an informal basketball scrimmage. I've yet to participate.

"It wasn't him," the secretary says.

"You then, Rachel?"

"Ha. No. I found him like that."

"Then who killed the kid?" gym teacher asks, looking around.

"Not sure," I say. "Maybe someone else, like us?"

They both shake their heads. "Doubtful," gym teacher says.

"Listen, can you call 911 again? I left my phone in the car, you know, Career Day . . . didn't want it interrupting. Tell them the situation. Stay in an alcove in case this isn't over. I'm going back to my wife and children. First, I'll check the rest of the school."

"You need a hand?" the gym teacher asks.

"Are you comfortable with a pistol?"

"Absolutely," he answers.

"Okay if we leave you here alone?" I ask the secretary, while handing the gym teacher my handgun.

"I'm fine here," she answers.

We cautiously make our way through the halls. We reach a body, a young man.

"You know him?" I ask the gym teacher.

"No," he shakes his head. "I thought he was with the other two, part of the . . . I don't know what to call them. Attackers? Shooters?"

I take a quick look over the body. He doesn't look like the other two. He's wearing blue jeans and a T-shirt. I check for a pulse. The secretary was correct. He's dead. There's plenty of blood. Gunshot wound to the temple, my guess would be self-inflicted based on the stippling and fouling of the tissue. But he doesn't have any weapons. No pistol, no AR, not even a knife. Odd. Kind of hard to shoot yourself in the head without a gun. Maybe someone picked it up?

In a matter of minutes, we've covered the entire school. There are no other hostiles. When we reach the hall intersecting where we left the secretary, the gym teacher says he'll go over and check on her and find out when the police should arrive.

I make my way back toward Mrs. Jenkins's classroom, wishing I had my phone so I could call Georgia, tell her what's happening. I don't want to scare her. It's not likely she'd shoot first and ask questions later, but . . .

As I reach the alcove to Mrs. Jenkins's room, I slow down considerably.

"Georgia, Georgia," I stage whisper, then try a little louder.

Very quietly, she says, "Sam?"

"It's me. I think it's over."

"I don't think . . . with the blood . . . the children," she says haltingly. "I don't think they should come out this door. Are the police here yet?"

"I don't know. I'm putting the carbine down and getting on my knees. They'll be here shortly, I'm sure. The school secretary, I met up with her, she was calling to update them."

"What should I do?"

"Put your gun away. Stay with our children. Everything will be fine."

A loud crash sounds from the other end of the building, followed by a second, closer crash—one of the emergency exits.

"They're here. I love you," I say, as I skid the rifle away from me and drop to my knees, hands on my head.

"Don't move. Don't you move!"

No fewer than half a dozen weapons are trained on me. I'm pushed violently to the ground. I turn my head and throw up my forearm, barely breaking my fall. At least my nose didn't land first.

"I'm Sam Mitchell. I'm a parent. My children— "

"Shut up, scumbag."

Pain rushes through my back, then my head. I feel myself losing consciousness. A far away voice says, "Stop. Stop. He's not the shooter. Stop. He's . . . "

Chapter 6

Georgia

"*Stop it now!* He's my husband. He's not one of them. He stopped them!" With the door cracked open, still hiding my body, I yell at the top of my lungs.

"Ma'am, you're safe now."

"No kidding, you idiot. I'm safe because *my husband*, Dr. Sam Mitchell, *the one you're beating up*, stopped them."

"I'm recording this." Mrs. Jenkins is pushing at me, sticking the phone through the slightly open door and into the hallway where Sam is now lying still. They've stopped hitting him.

"Those fascist pigs can't beat an innocent man like that," Mrs. Jenkins says indignantly.

"Mrs. Jenkins? Is that you?"

"Of course it's me. And this is going to be you on YouTube if you don't get your act together."

"Yes, ma'am. It's me, Timmy Arnold. You taught me."

"Oh, yes. I remember you. Bit of a troublemaker, weren't you? I heard a rumor you were with our police department. Truthfully, I wouldn't have thought you'd end up on the right side of the law. Of course, beating an innocent man like that . . . "

"Let me check on my husband," I demand.

"No, ma'am. You'll need to stay in there for now. We have an ambulance on the way."

"My husband is a doctor. I know what to do. Let me check on him now." I use my best calm voice.

"Arnold, the building is secure," a loud voice booms from down the hall.

"We have a bus on the way?" he asks the booming voice.

"Yep. About two minutes out."

"Affirmative." He turns to me and says, "Step on out here, ma'am. Watch yourself. There's quite a bit of blood and a dead guy there."

"No kidding," I mumble.

I quickly assess Sam. He's breathing fine. There's a knot on the back of his head where he was hit with the rifle butt. There's so much blood on him from the guy earlier, I can't tell if he's cut and bleeding.

"Sam?" No response. "Sam, honey? Can you hear me? Just lie still. The ambulance is on its way. You're going to be fine."

Soon, Sam is loaded up and on his way to the hospital. I'm prevented from going with him, forced to stay to be interviewed. First by the Groyver City Police, then the county sheriff department, and finally the highway patrol. I'm told to expect the FBI tomorrow.

The city police and state trooper both give me a strong talking to about bringing a weapon into a Gun-Free Zone. They also confiscate my pistol, even though it wasn't fired or used. I'm told Sam's pistol was taken also, along with the pistol being held by Rachel Wheeler. She took it from Principal Skinner's office. I was terribly upset to learn that Kent Skinner was one of three killed. Three adults. No children, thankfully. I have no doubt my husband is the reason more weren't killed.

"Mrs. Mitchell?"

"Yes?"

"You and your children can go. I just heard from the hospital. Your husband is waking up," a sheriff deputy, the one who interviewed me, says.

"Okay, thank you."

"Uh, you know, it might be best for me to give you a ride. There're already quite a few news people here. Don't know how they got here so quick. My guess is, it's going to get worse, especially when people hear about how you two stopped the killers."

I cringe. "Any way we could keep that quiet? We don't need that kind of— "

"Yes, ma'am. I know. But your children's teacher . . . she's already been blasting social media. Even made a video about her ordeal. You and your husband are mentioned many times."

I sigh. Of course she did. I had no idea a woman close to retirement age would even realize the power of social media. Personally, I can't stand it.

"Could I take my car, but maybe you could follow us? Just to make sure we're not bothered?"

"Absolutely. I need to go talk with your husband anyway. Usually the sheriff would be handing these interviews himself, but he's out of town, hustling back now so he can handle the news media."

"Deputy?"

"Sandoval, ma'am. Ray Sandoval."

"Deputy Sandoval, thank you for your kindness. I appreciate it. Please don't for a minute think it changes the fact my husband was beaten. He was on the ground, not a threat, and beaten."

"Understood, ma'am. Not to shift the blame, but you should know, that was state and city police. Deputy Richardson and I were at the other door. If we had been there, that stuff wouldn't have happened."

I give him a long hard look, then hug my kids tight to me. "We're ready to go now."

Chapter 7

Sam

I move slightly. Ugh. That was a mistake. To say my head hurts would be an understatement. Do I have a hangover? Did I drink and blackout? It's not just my head. My back, my right arm, the backs of both legs—why do I hurt like this? *Whiskey.* I don't remember drinking, but I definitely feel like I've been.

I close my eyes again.

"Dr. Mitchell, there you are. Good to have you back with us."

Her voice startles me. I jump, resulting in another explosion, starting at my toes and blowing off the top of my head. Figuratively, of course.

"Yeah. I'm here," my whisper comes out as a croak.

"Excellent. I'll find Doctor Monroe. I know he'll be happy to hear you're awake."

"Mm-hmm."

A few minutes later, Doctor Monroe, whom I know from professional events and dinner one time at his house, booms, "Well, there you are, Sam. Wondered when you'd be joining us again."

"Hey, Jackson," I croak.

"So, old sport, there's a whole herd of people waiting to talk with you. I hear Georgia is on her way also. I figured we'd let her see you first. Of course, that's provided the state trooper lurking in the hall allows it. Thought you might need to, you know, get your stories straight." He gives me a pronounced wink.

Get our stories straight? For the life of me, I can't even figure out why I feel so bad. "Were we in a car accident? Are they okay?"

"What's that you say?"

I clear my throat and try again. "A car accident? I feel pretty terrible but don't know why. Was it an accident? Are Georgia and the kids okay?"

"A car accident? Nope. You don't remember?"

Do I remember? My head hurts so bad, I can't even try to think about what happened. I allow myself to drift off.

Chapter 8

Georgia

Deputy Sandoval, along with the second deputy, run interference to get us to our car. I can't believe how many people are here. The shooting only happened a short time ago. And Groyver isn't exactly a metropolis.

The hospital isn't much better. People are everywhere outside. Some even seem to know our names, calling for me, Chloe, and Willie. Deputy Sandoval, once again, does an excellent job of intervening.

When we get to Sam's room, the highway patrol officer who interviewed me at the school is there. I didn't like him much at the school. While he wasn't one of the officers who beat Sam, he also made it clear he wasn't planning on condemning the assault.

"Georgia," he says, raising his hand to stop me, "I'll let you know when you can see Sam."

I bristle at the way he says Sam, like he knows my husband.

"How about this, Officer Peters, I'll let you know when you can see my husband. And when you do see him, you'll address him as either Lieutenant Commander Mitchell or Dr. Mitchell. He's more than earned the right to be addressed properly and with respect. And while we're at it, you can call me Dr. Mitchell also. Because, Officer Peters, I can assure you, *we're* not on a first name basis."

"Now see here, *Dr. Mitchell*," he sneers, "that's not— "

"Lighten up, Dylan," Deputy Sandoval says, stepping between Officer Peters and me. "You'll get your opportunity to talk to him. Right now, I'm taking his wife and children in so they can see him."

"You know that's not how we do things, Ray. We interview all suspects— "

"Suspect? How exactly is my husband a suspect?"

"I'm sorry, Dr. Mitchell, I misspoke. He's not an actual suspect, we just want to make sure to get his version of events before there's any dilution."

"Dilution? Oh, you mean like so we don't match up our stories? So I can be sure to point out to him that he was hit in the back by one of your officers and a second one wacked him in the head. Then they took turns on his extremities. You mean getting our stories together like that?" I do my best to keep something resembling a smile on my face and my voice at an even keel.

"Now, now, that's not at all what I meant."

"Dylan . . . " Deputy Sandoval says, warning filling his voice.

"Fine," Officer Peters snaps. "But this is on you, Ray. You think the sheriff is going to be happy when he hears about you interfering?"

"You think the sheriff is going to be happy when he sees the results of your guys' handiwork?" I ask.

Deputy Sandoval represses a smile. "Let's go, Dr. Mitchell." He turns to my children, both wide eyed from my exchange with Officer Peters. Oops. Maybe I should've toned it down a bit. Not that they haven't witnessed me freak out before.

"I bet you two are ready to see your dad," he says with a smile. "I have no doubt he's ready to see you."

I pull Chloe and Willie close to me as we stride down the hall, tight on Deputy Sandoval's heels.

Sam is asleep. They've cleaned him up. He's no longer covered in someone else's blood, but he's still a mess. There's a cut across his eyebrow and bruises on his arms. Two fingers and his left hand have been bandaged. His right index finger is in a splint.

Chloe gasps, startling him awake. He scrunches up his face and sucks in a deep breath, then slowly opens his eyes.

"Hey," he heaves, sounding terrible.

I go to his side, reaching for him. "Hey, yourself."

"You guys are okay?" he asks.

"We're fine. You took care of everything. We weren't in danger."

"You weren't in the car with me?"

"What?"

"The car? Wasn't there an accident?"

"A car accident? No . . . Do you remember what happened, Sam?"

Sam squeezes his eyes shut.

"Dad," Willie says, gently touching his arm, "there were bad guys at the school. You stopped them. You're a hero."

"A hero?"

"Yeah, Dad," Chloe says, standing next to Willie. "Don't you remember?"

"I'm . . . I'm not sure."

Chapter 9

Sam

Over the course of several hours, the events started to return, including remembering the police using me as a punching bag. Someone with the city police assured me it was a case of mistaken identity and that they were terribly sorry. Another guy, a complete tool from the highway patrol, implied it was completely my fault since I should've stayed out of it and let them do their job.

Deputy Ray Sandoval, with the county sheriff department, made sure that guy got out of the room. I think he could tell I was recovering pretty quickly and was ready to bounce out of that bed and kick his—

"Hey, Dad. You about ready?" Willie interrupts my reflection over yesterday.

"Sure am. More than ready. Looking forward to getting out of here and back home."

"Me too," Chloe says. "It was kind of fun to stay in the hotel last night, but I miss my room."

"Um, folks," Deputy Sandoval, here to escort us home, clears his throat. "I think it might be a good idea for you to stay in a hotel again tonight. Your house is under siege. One of our deputies just did a drive by to check it out, and the media's camped in your yard."

"Camped in our yard?" Georgia sputters.

"Not actually camped, but they're there. Dozens of them. Just like in the hospital parking lot."

"What do you think we should do?" I ask.

"I'm not sure. You could give a press conference, maybe that'd satisfy them. I know the sheriff and the powers that be in the town asked you to hold off on that a day or two."

"Humph," Georgia huffs. "Only because they don't want their handiwork being so evident."

Besides the city and state police, we've had visits from the sheriff, the mayor, someone from city council, and a call from the governor—all under the pretense of making sure I was okay. You know, so I don't sue the pants off them for beating me to a near pulp.

While none have directly said it, all have implied they'll bend over backward to prevent a lawsuit. I haven't even thought about suing. While I fully feel they treated me as a criminal, part of me also understands. Someone shot up the school. Someone killed the principal and two teachers. The two officers who spearheaded my beating have children at the school.

"Same hotel as last night?" Chloe asks.

"How about a different one?" I say. "Let's go over to Gillette, stay at the one with the really nice swimming pool. How's that sound?"

The children both give an enthusiastic yes. "Gillette?" Georgia asks.

"Yeah," Deputy Sandoval agrees with a nod. "Might give you a little more privacy."

"We need to go by the house, get some more clothes," Georgia says.

"Can you make do with what you have?" the deputy asks. "Or maybe . . . there's a SuperMart in Gillette. I could pop over and pick up a few things for you."

Georgia and I share a look. I shrug. "Okay, Deputy," she says.

"Ray. How about you guys start calling me Ray."

Chapter 10

Georgia

The children loved the pool with a lazy river and several slides. Yesterday, we went back to Groyver for a press conference where the mayor gave Sam and me a key to the city. Symbolically, anyway. They still need to make the plaques to present to us.

Sam is healing well. He still has a headache and bruising but is doing better physically. The broken pinkie finger on his right hand is an annoyance more than anything, at least that's what he says. The cuts on his left hand, which happened when he was taking out the first guy, are very minor. He said he didn't even realize he'd cut himself until Doctor Pompous, also known as Jackson Monroe, told him.

Sam and I suffered through a dinner with Jackson Monroe. He was arrogant and terribly condescending. The entire evening, I racked my brain trying to figure out who he reminded me of. It finally hit me. Charles Emerson Winchester III from *M*A*S*H*. Jackson Monroe even has the Boston accent. Funny thing, Jackson was raised in Cleveland.

Sam has had a couple of nightmares. We both know it's to be expected, but it still scared our children.

Ray was able to get the media moved down the road, so they're no longer right on our lawn. Our neighbors, while grateful for what Sam did, are less than impressed with the national attention we're now receiving.

We've had a slew of phone calls from people we've known through the years. People who were friends, acquaintances, and even a few who we weren't exactly friendly with. Our church pastor has tried to visit a few times but turned back due to the craziness. While, like the neighbors, I'm so thankful Sam did what he did, I'm done with our fifteen minutes of fame. I'm ready for our regular lives to return.

Mrs. Jenkins's videos of Sam's beating went viral, and she's definitely enjoying the celebrity status from it. After the press conference today, the city's attorney met with us. They've asked us to sign a paper saying we won't sue the city in exchange for Sam's medical costs being covered, after the insurance pays their part, plus a lump sum payment for his pain and suffering. We heard the state's attorney will have a similar offer.

Sam and I briefly discussed it. He says he'll let them pay the medical bills since he was uninjured except for the small cuts on his hand until they went to work on him. But he doesn't want any cash. He doesn't feel that'd be right since he can somewhat relate to the guys and what they were emotionally experiencing.

Me . . . I want to sue until the city goes bankrupt. I want the city and state police to be held accountable. I especially want that weasel Dylan Peters to lose his job. I think Sam and I are going to compromise and suggest the city and state start scholarship funds in the names of Principal Kent Skinner and the two teachers who were murdered.

The two officers who assaulted Sam are on administrative leave, pending charges from the district attorney. With the video evidence, there's little doubt they'll be charged. They'll probably lose their jobs. Sam, again, thinks that's too much. Says he'll be a witness of the defense, or some such thing. Me, I think they should be fired and blackballed from ever working in law enforcement. Even being a security guard at the mall should be off limits.

Besides the whole beating controversy, there's additional controversy over the shooters. In addition to the guy Sam knifed outside Mrs. Jenkins's room and the one he shot in the next hallway over, there was a third guy, assumed to be with the assailants.

A guy Sam didn't kill. Rachel Wheeler, school secretary and the only other person who we know was armed besides me, also didn't kill him. She said he was dead when she found him.

The other two guys were dressed for combat and in their early to midthirties. The third guy was in jeans and T-shirt. He was young, graduated from Groyver High School last year. And that's not all, when the police went to deliver the news to his mom, she was dead too.

The working theory is he somehow hooked up with the two guys in black, killed his mom, and then met them at the school so they could kill as many as possible. The boy had gone to school there, kindergarten through fifth grade. Mrs. Jenkins was even his third-grade teacher. Of course, she said she always knew he was bad news and wasn't at all surprised by him being involved in this.

Sam killed the other two guys, but who killed the boy? That's the question no one can answer. Sam thought the gunshot looked self-inflicted, but there wasn't a gun around the boy. And even more disturbing, no one seems to be trying to answer the question of who killed him.

Rachel Wheeler along with the gym teacher, Michael Sewell, were both interviewed by a national news show yesterday. They made a big deal about the boy—about finding him dead. The interviewer kept redirecting them from the dead boy to the fact that Principal Skinner carried a gun on his ankle and had a gun in his office in a school. And, *gasp*, Sam and I took guns into the school. After all, it's a Gun-Free Zone.

Michael pointed out that the killers didn't adhere to the sign. And he pointed out we didn't use our guns. Sam killed them with his knife and the AR the first dead guy had. His points were glazed over and dismissed.

I'm getting ready for bed when our house phone rings. We're totally old school and still keep a landline. Mainly because our cell service is hit or miss, and Sam needs to be available for emergencies.

Sam takes the call in the bedroom. I eavesdrop while putting on my moisturizer.

"Hey, Jeff."

His business partner. Probably checking in, confirming the plan of when Sam and I will be back to work. A week from Monday. We've decided we're taking the rest of this week and next week off.

Jeff took care of seeing some of the patients Sam had scheduled. But the remaining less urgent cases have been pushed back, with the promise they'll be scheduled as soon as Sam is back. All of my patients are also being rescheduled. I spoke with our office manager, Gloria, today, and she was working on rearranging things. Maybe she didn't relay the latest info to Jeff.

"No, that's fine," Sam says into the phone. "He seems to be a good guy. He's the one that invited me to play basketball. Remember me telling you about that?"

A pause. "Yep. Exactly. Did you take his number? Okay, good. Hey, I'm upstairs and it looks like someone has run off with the notepad again. Can you text me the number?"

"Thanks, Jeff. Gloria told you our plans?"

I stop listening and start brushing my teeth. The whir of the electric toothbrush makes it impossible to continue my eavesdropping.

Sam wraps his arms around me, nuzzling my neck.

"You must be feeling better," I say.

"Still sore and have a small headache. It's not too bad."

He kisses my neck, sending chills down my entire left side.

Our eyes meet in the mirror.

"You keep that up and we may have to test just how well you are," my voice comes out huskier than usual.

Even after twenty-seven years together, Sam still takes my breath away. Not only with his touch but his complete presence. He's handsome—ruggedly handsome some might say. With a strong jaw, perfect nose, hazel eyes, and a dimple on the right side, he's adorable.

He's wearing his hair longer these days. Not a lot longer, but more length than when he was in the Navy. Dark blond with streaks—silver streaks. If he goes a few days without shaving, his beard is predominately gray. To be expected at almost fifty. Personally, I think it's terribly sexy. He's aged amazingly well and is even hotter now than when we were in college.

He didn't catch my eye when we first met. We had classes together for three years before we even spoke. I thought he was just another pretty face and didn't really have any desire to get to know him. It wasn't until the summer before our senior year, when we did a special clerkship together, that we got to know each other.

Sam had already decided he was going into the Navy. It was the only way he could afford medical school. Premed was paid for via scholarships and his dad's life insurance.

When I found out about his Navy plans, I tried to push him away. Even though what we had was probably just a fling, I knew I didn't want to be a Navy wife. How could I? That'd be too difficult for my own medical practice. And I had to become a doctor. My mom was counting on me.

A vibration on my backside brings me back to the present.

"Oh, baby," I laugh.

"Oops. Text. Forgot I had the ringer off. Jeff was going to send the gym teacher's number. He called the service, and Jeff ended up talking to him but didn't want to give out our private number, thought we might be upset after the interview he and the secretary did."

"Michael and Rachel."

"Huh?"

"Their names. Not gym teacher and secretary."

One of Sam's faults, he remembers faces but not names. A second fault, the cell phone. He's always turning the ringer off and missing calls or leaving the phone in a different room. When he's on call, I'm constantly reminding him of his phone. It's to the point the service now calls our home phone first, then my cell, and finally tries his cell.

"Okay, sure. Michael and Rachel. You know, it's pretty late. I'll call Michael tomorrow. Now, where were we?"

Chapter 11

After breakfast, Georgia is loading the dishwasher while I wipe the table.

"You call Michael?" she asks.

"Michael?"

She gives me a look, then says, "The gym teacher."

"Oh . . . that Michael. I thought you meant . . . never mind. I'll call him."

The phone goes straight to voicemail. I leave a message with my cell number. As I start to disconnect, I decide to leave the home phone number also. Sometimes I miss the cell phone calls.

A few minutes later, my cell starts buzzing.

"Sam Mitchell," I answer.

"Hey, Doc, it's Michael Sewell. Thanks for returning my call."

"Yep, sure. Saw your interview."

"Yeah, that was quite a show. Kept getting steered in a different direction. Sorry it didn't paint you better. You know you're a hero. Don't care what that network twit implied."

"It did seem she had a bit of an agenda for her interview. Saw her torn apart on another channel for how she handled it. You doing any more interviews?"

"Not me. Not Rachel either. You?"

"Not if I can help it. Been getting calls at my office from people, but so far we've been fortunate they haven't found our private numbers."

"How'd you manage that?"

"My business partner. He set up our cells and home phone through an alias. Says it's better that way so patients aren't calling at all hours. I'm pretty thankful for it now. They did find our house, not exactly sure how."

"Yeah, it's a little crazy the way they are. So the reason I've called, have you had anything strange happen?"

"You're kidding, right?"

He gives a small laugh. "Let me clarify. Rachel and I both think someone has been in our homes."

"Reporters?"

"Maybe. I don't know. We also feel like we're being watched."

I'm pretty sure I roll my eyes. "Yeah, us too. Reporters are everywhere, definitely watching us. Probably the same for you."

"This is different. The reporters are bold and in our face. This . . . this is more of a shadow thing."

"Shadow thing?"

"Yeah, like I know someone's there, but I can't catch them. You have anything like that?"

"No, can't say I do."

"Okay, that's good. Maybe we're just paranoid." He gives another small laugh. "I'm going to take off for a few days, go see my girl in Rapid City. Maybe we'll shoot over to Deadwood and recuperate. Kent Skinner and I were pretty good friends, went to college together. He brought me here, ya know."

"I didn't know. I'm sorry for your loss."

"Yeah. It sucks for sure. Rachel is pretty upset also. She's good friends with his wife, so she knew him well too."

"How's his wife holding up? There going to be a service?"

"She's doing okay. Yes, a week from Saturday. His brother is overseas, wanted to give him time to get home. I'll be back in time for the service. Probably be a full three-ring circus with the media vultures. Think you'll be there?"

"Yes, probably. How about the other teachers that were killed? Do you know about their arrangements?"

"Their families aren't from Groyver. They'll have services in their hometowns. We'll do something for them here also. Rachel is going to spearhead it."

"That sounds good. I wish . . . " I pause my thought. I don't want to tell him how much I wish I had realized what was happening sooner. Maybe I could've prevented one or both of the teachers from dying. Kent was killed first, but the others . . . maybe I could've . . . "Will you let me know?"

"Sure I will. Talk to you later, Doctor. Oh, and seriously, keep your eyes open. You're probably right about it being nothing, but . . . I don't know. Things don't feel right."

"Okay, sure. Things will be fine. I really think it's the media or paparazzi or whatever they are."

"Probably so." He sighs.

With that, we disconnect. I get it, Michael and the secretary—what's her name?—feeling suspicious of everyone. It's a normal response to a traumatic situation. I'm feeling a bit of it myself. Not to the point I think there's a boogeyman behind every corner, but I get it.

Georgia and I spend the day hiding out at home with the children. We play board games and watch movies. We purposely avoid the television and internet.

The craziness of the media is kept at bay by the homeowner's association patrol, plus the sheriff and city patrols. While we don't live in a gated community, we do have a rather strong HOA presence, including hired security. Usually, they're just monitoring to make sure a camp trailer isn't parked in someone's front yard. Now, they're earning their keep. Ray was able to convince Officer Tool, or whatever his name is, to put extra patrol cars in the neighborhood. I think it was mainly done so we'll stick by our informal agreement to not sue the city for beating the tar out of me.

Shortly after supper, our home phone rings. "I'll get it," Chloe yells.

"Not today, sweetie," Georgia says. "Dad and I will answer the phone until things calm down around here."

Even though the media hasn't found our number yet, we know that could change at any time.

"Hello?" Georgia says. "Rachel? Rachel, what's wrong?"

Chapter 12

Georgia

"Rachel, I can't understand you."

"It's Michael. He's . . . oh, Dr. Mitchell, it's so terrible. He's dead."

I fumble with the desk chair, trying to find a seat. What'd she say?

"What's going on?" Sam asks.

I hold up a finger. "Rachel, I'm going to have Sam get on the extension. Is that okay?"

"Y-yes," she gulps.

Sam tells Chloe to go back and watch the movie, we'll be right back in, as he heads toward our bedroom.

A click, then, "I'm here. What's going on?"

"Oh, Doctor. I had just talked to him."

"To who?" Sam asks, voice laced with impatience.

"To Michael! He's dead. Michael is dead."

Sam is silent for several seconds, while Rachel cries.

"How?" he finally asks.

"Car wreck. On his way to see his girlfriend. He lost control or something. It's so terrible."

"Oh, Rachel, I'm so sorry," I say.

"Me t-too." She quietly cries for several seconds, takes a deep breath, and whispers, "It wasn't an accident. They did it."

"What'd you say?" Sam asks.

A little louder, she says, "He told me he talked to you. He gave me this number. Your cell number too. Tried that first, but you didn't answer."

"Sorry, had the ringer off."

She continues like she didn't hear him. "He said he told you about our homes being broken into. About the people following us."

"Sam?" I ask.

"I'll catch you up after we're off the phone, Georgia. Rachel, I . . . I'm sorry. He did tell me, but I thought . . . I think it's probably the media people. I wouldn't be surprised if one of them was in your home. They're rabid when after a story. And they'd definitely follow you."

"It's not them," she snaps. "This is something different. We both know we were followed. Michael—it wasn't an accident. They killed him. And now . . . now I think they'll try and kill me."

"Oh, Rachel," I say, "I know you're upset over Michael. And after the shooting and the news media, we're all on edge. Would you like me to see if Ray—Deputy Ray Sandoval— can stop by? He can check your place, make sure everything is okay."

"You think he would? I filed a report after the break-in, but they acted like I was crazy. I'm not crazy, Dr. Mitchell. I'm not."

I choose not to address her mental state. While I agree she's not crazy, I suspect she's overreacting. I get that. I'm totally on edge also. If I hear a loud noise, my startle response is on overdrive.

"I'll call Ray, have him come over," Sam says. "What's your address?"

She rattles off the address, which I copy down, figuring Sam doesn't have a pen or paper by the bed. Oh, they're supposed to be one there, but he's always picking it up and walking away with one, the other, or both.

"Okay, Rachel, just sit tight. He'll be there soon. Oh, what's your phone number?" Sam asks.

I interrupt and say, "It's on our caller ID."

"You have it?" Rachel asks. "Can you make sure?"

I read back the number, and she confirms it. After we hang up, I go to the bedroom.

"Terrible about Michael," I say, as Sam pulls me close. "Want to call Ray?"

"Already did. He's heading to her place. He already knew about Michael but will try to get more details so he can put her mind at ease."

"What was she talking about?"

Sam spends several minutes clarifying their fears of the break-ins and both thinking they were being followed.

"Okay . . . " I say. "And what do you think?"

"Sounds a little crazy. Paranoid. It's likely just a response to the shooting. My guess is most of the other teachers, and maybe the students, are having similar feelings. Just like us. Just like our kids. We're all a little on edge."

"Exactly. We've been through a lot. Everyone at the school has. Even our entire town. It'd be normal for people to lose it a little. Of course, Mrs. Jenkins seems to be handling things just fine." I smirk.

That woman. A cowering fool when the trouble was real, chastising Sam and me for wanting to do something to stop the attack, thinking her staple gun was a match for an AR. If we hadn't been there . . . I give an involuntary shudder as I think of what might have happened. My children would've been sitting ducks.

"Mrs. Jenkins is definitely a horse of a different color," Sam says. "Thought that the first day we met her. You know that."

I nod and say, "So you don't think there's anything to the paranoia? Michael's accident was just that, an accident? Rachel is freaking out over nothing?"

"Like you said, the last few days have been hard. Ray will check things out. Maybe he'll suggest a hotel for a few days. He said he'll call me later, give me an update."

We're in bed. I'm almost asleep when I hear the buzz of Sam's cell phone as it vibrates on his nightstand.

Chapter 13

Sam

"Sam. Sam, your phone," Georgia says, shaking me back to consciousness. Ugh. My head still hurts.

"What's going on?" I croak.

"Your phone."

"My phone," I repeat dumbly. Oh.

"It's stopped now, but you had a call. Thought you were going to turn the ringer back on?"

"Forgot."

I rub my shoulder where she was shaking me. Another painful spot. Those guys got in some good jabs. At least I feel better . . . mostly. I've yet to watch the video Mrs. Jenkins put out for the world. Don't know if I can handle watching myself get beat up.

"Who was on the phone?" Georgia asks.

"Let me check." I'm reaching for it, as it once again starts its nightstand dance.

"Deputy Ray," I say aloud before answering. "Yes?"

"Hey, Doc. Sorry to call you so late. Thought you might want an update."

"Sure, that's fine. Mind if I put you on speaker so Georgia can hear also?"

"No problem."

"Okay, go ahead."

"Hey, Dr. Mitchell."

"Georgia. Please call me Georgia."

"Sure, Georgia. Anyway, I just left Rachel Wheeler's place. Did my due diligence and checked things out. Everything seemed fine. I went over the police reports she and Michael filed regarding the break-ins. Nothing was taken. I agree it was probably an overzealous reporter.

Michael's accident seems legit, nothing suspicious. He was probably going too fast and lost control. The roads were dry, so nothing else really makes sense. Maybe an animal ran in front of him and he tried to dodge it, but there's no concrete evidence one way or another.

"Okay, she's paranoid," I say.

"Yeah . . . except maybe she's not. When I was leaving, I thought I saw someone. I tried to get close enough to confront them but wasn't able to."

"Another reporter?" Georgia asks.

"Most likely. But why hide like that? There were a few reporters out in the open. One even tried to interview me. So it just seemed odd."

"What's the plan?" I ask.

"I'm going to hang out for a bit. I'm in my work truck. I'll wait and see if they come back around. I figure the sheriff logo might be a deterrent at least."

"Rachel didn't want to go to a hotel?" Georgia asks.

"We talked about it. She said she'd feel even more exposed in a public place."

"Understandable," Georgia agrees.

"Anyway, pretty sure it's nothing, but I'll hang out a bit to make sure. I'll let you know tomorrow if anything comes of it."

"Sounds good. Thanks for doing this, Ray. Goodnight."

I disconnect and snuggle back into bed.

"You think there was someone?" Georgia asks.

I shrug. "Probably media, like Ray said. Maybe just looking for a different angle, seeing if they could get closer or something."

"Probably so."

Georgia scooches over next to me, draping her arm across my chest. After a few minutes, her breathing becomes rhythmic.

I try to follow suit but am now wide awake. Replaying the school attack, the killing I did, the mystery of the boy shooter—who, as far as we know, didn't shoot anyone. He didn't even have a gun on him. How'd he kill his mom? I haven't heard. I'll ask Ray about this tomorrow.

Part of me thinks I should feel worse about killing the other two. The two in black have yet to be identified. Mostly, I just wish I would've killed them quicker. Maybe one or both teachers could've been spared. I try not to think about this. I know I should be grateful more people weren't killed or hurt. I'm glad I had the Marine training so I had an inkling of what to do.

Will my new status as a killer cost me patients? Maybe. Of course, it's just as likely to bring new people in—the ones who are rather macabre and fascinated by killers and death. Lord knows every population has plenty of those. Groyver is no exception.

Chapter 14

Georgia

It's early afternoon when the house phone rings. Sam is playing Monopoly with the children. I glance at the caller ID, don't recognize the number, and choose to let the machine pick up. We're still old school, with an actual answering machine, circa 1995, so I can hear the person leaving the message and decide to pick up or not.

A pause after the greeting, then, "Yeah, it's Ray Sandoval. Wondering if you've heard from Rachel Wheeler today."

"Ray, it's Georgia," I say, after picking up the handset.

"Hey, Georgia. Have you talked to Rachel today?"

"She called earlier, thanking us for sending you over."

"What time was that?" Ray asks.

"Nine o'clock, almost on the dot. I remember thinking she probably waited to call, you know, nine being the old etiquette for acceptable calling times." I give a small laugh. "Why are you asking?"

"I dropped by to check on her, only she isn't around."

"Okay. Maybe she went to the store or somewhere."

"Maybe. But . . . I looked in her window, the curtain was open a sliver. Some of the furniture looked out of place."

"Out of place?"

"A piece toppled over, the others scooted out of place. Not like it was last night when I was here. I checked the door. It was unlocked. I then decided I had probable cause to enter. She's not here, but things look . . . anyway. I was just wondering if she may have called you, given you any idea of her plans today."

"No, she didn't tell me anything like that."

"Okay. If you do hear from her, ask her to call me."

"You putting out some sort of missing person alert?"

He pauses. There's a rustling sound, then very softly he says, "Can't get any traction on that."

"What's that mean?"

"Protocol."

"Protocol," I parrot.

"Exactly."

What's he telling me? He's being terribly cryptic. "Someone's there so you can't speak freely?"

"That's right."

"So . . . you have rules to follow for missing persons, and you can't waver from them?"

"Correct."

"You agree with those rules?"

"Not necessarily, not in this instance."

"But you're following them anyway."

"No choice."

"Okay . . . " I leave it hanging out there, thinking he may elaborate. When he doesn't, I say, "We'll let you know if we hear from her. Oh, do you have her cell number?"

"I do. Tried it. Off or out of service area. Goes straight to voicemail."

"All right. When she turns up, will you let us know or ask her to call?"

Chapter 15

Sam

We spent yesterday hanging out around the house. We watched movies and played games. I also spent some time in our basement gym. We never did hear from Rachel. I called Ray at about 7:00 last night. He had yet to make contact with her. It was still too soon to declare her an official missing person.

If it wasn't for the overturned furniture, we'd think she just took off for a few days. The furniture, and the fact her phone goes straight to voicemail, is concerning.

I'm beginning to wonder if there isn't something to her paranoia.

Ray must agree. We talked a few minutes ago, and he said her missing person case is now official. Some kind of evidence showed up, allowing them to escalate it.

"You ready to go?" Georgia asks.

"Yep. Just let me get my shoes on. Are the kids ready?"

"They are. They're excited to get out of the house. Even if we're just going to Jeff's place."

"I have to admit, I'm excited too. Feels like we've been holed up for days."

"Sam Mitchell, are you implying you haven't enjoyed our quality time together?" Georgia gives me one of her winning smiles while flipping her shoulder-length chestnut hair.

"You know that's not the case," I say, standing up and opening up my arms. She steps into my embrace. The top of her head is the perfect height for me to rest my chin, if I bend my knees slightly. She's five foot four to my six foot three. She calls herself short. I like to think of her as fun-size.

I inhale her scent. Coconut shampoo with a hint of orange, her body spray. Yummy.

"What's going on here, Mister?" she teases. "It's time for us to leave, not . . . " She raises her eyebrows at me. "Oh, I know. I guess our quality time together these last few days is . . . stirring things up."

Stirring things up. That's one way to put it. I stifle a sigh. We came too close to dying. Too close to not being able to have this intimacy. While we haven't had any issues in the romance department, I've decided I'm going to make sure Georgia knows she's loved. Wanted. After all these years, she's my one and only.

"Okay, we'd better take off. But tonight . . . " I kiss her, giving her a sample of my intentions for tonight.

Chapter 16

"You look wonderful," Tawny Ridgely gushes, "so well rested."

"Thank you," I say, accepting her hug and a kiss on each cheek. A native Wyomingite, Tawny spent several weeks touring Italy and now chooses to embrace her inner Italian. Her words, not mine.

I like Tawny and enjoy spending time with both her and Jeff, but we don't really have much in common. Oh, we're both world travelers. She for pleasure and me whenever I could join Sam at an overseas posting. Sometimes that was a short trip for only a few days and we'd sneak in a little sightseeing. Other times, I stayed for an entire tour.

Tawny and I are both passionate about our work. She for volunteer causes, me helping to build the practice our husbands have partnered. Where Sam is 25 percent partner, I'm an employee. It's still a good deal for us, but a better deal for Jeff.

Jeff and Tawny didn't have children, so they enjoy spoiling ours. It's kind of nice for Chloe and Willie. They're treated very much like loved grandchildren, even though Tawny is only a few months older than me.

Sam and I thought we'd be like Tawny and Jeff—childless. We tried for years, with no success. When I turned forty, we gave up. Figured it just wasn't meant to be. I was heartbroken.

All I ever wanted was to be a mom. Going to med school was not my idea. I wanted to marry my high school sweetheart, settle down, and make babies. Lots of babies.

My mom wouldn't hear of it. She wanted "more" for me. What she meant was she wanted more for herself. It was her dream to be a doctor. All through high school, she planned on going to med school, then doing something noble, like Doctors Without Borders. Instead, she got pregnant. With me. Her parents forced her to marry my dad. Mom told the story over and over and over. *Yes, Mom, I get it. I ruined your life. Thanks for sharing.*

When I was five, she went to the community college and became a Licensed Practical Nurse—an LPN. She hated being a nurse, always felt it was beneath her. Bed pans, sponge baths, disgusting work, she used to say.

My mom was terribly bitter. Most of the bitterness was directed toward my dad, but there was enough to share with me. More than enough. Outwardly, it never seemed to bother him. Inwardly, I know it did. It had to. One time I tried to get him to open up, to complain about her to me. He flat refused. Said he made a vow to honor my mom, and he intended to keep that vow.

To appease her, I agreed to apply to the University of Washington. My boyfriend, Lyle, also applied. He was going for general studies and would later decide on a major. I was premed. We were both accepted.

Unbeknownst to me, UW was his second choice. I was his second choice. He had also applied to UCLA and was accepted. He left me in a hot minute, choosing California over Washington. Of course, he said we'd stay together and see each other on holidays. Didn't happen.

I was miserable the first year at UW. The only good thing, I had zero social life and mostly focused on my studies.

Sam was a freshman also. We never spoke. I still had zero desire to be a doctor. During my sophomore year, Mom hurt her back at work. She ended up on disability. My junior year I decided, if I had to be a doctor, I would specialize in sports medicine. I was always athletic. Even though I'm short, I played volleyball and basketball in high school. I never made first string but was varsity for both. I also ran track, doing quite well.

Sports medicine involves very little blood and doesn't have insane hours. Both a win in my book. My mom envisioned me as a surgeon. She wasn't impressed with my choice.

While the Navy paid for Sam's medical school, my mom's inheritance was paying for my schooling, both premed and on to medical school. Or so I thought.

"Can I get you something to drink?" Jeff asks, interrupting my reminiscing.

"I made a pitcher of sangria," Tawny says. At my look, she adds, "Don't worry. It's your kind. Perfect for the entire Mitchell family. I made a separate pitcher for Jeff and me, with the real stuff."

"You made mock sangria?"

"Sure. In some circles, I believe they'd call it fruit punch." She gives a bright, airy laugh. "But we're festive and going with sangria in honor of my upcoming trip to Spain."

I don't bother to mention, during my own trip to Madrid, one of the locals clued me in on sangria being a US custom which hasn't really caught on in Spain. They make it for the tourists but not the residents.

"Sounds delicious," I say instead.

Our visit is nice, having assorted tapas and a paella, made by their cook earlier in the day and reheated at the right time, to go along with the sangria.

We're about halfway through our twenty-minute drive home when Sam starts acting weird, looking in the mirrors and changing his speed. Slower, then faster, then slower again. When he turns on his right signal to take a turn we shouldn't be taking, I ask what's up.

"We're being followed," he answers tersely.

"The news people again? I thought maybe they'd given up when we didn't see them at our house earlier."

"Yeah, me too. Guess not."

"So . . . what are you doing?"

"Trying to lose them."

"Uh, Sam, don't you think they know where we live and can just wait there for us?"

His shoulders sag. "Maybe. Yeah, I guess you're right. Makes sense they'd know where Jeff lives and follow us from there."

I peer in my side mirror. "I think you lost them anyway."

He shrugs and resumes driving normally.

Chapter 17

Sam

Yep. I'm feeling pretty paranoid. And I'm really starting to understand Michael and Rachel. Yes, Georgia is probably right. It's a reporter. But it doesn't feel like that. It feels like someone's after us.

I haven't told Georgia, but someone was in the neighbor's backyard today. Not the neighbor, they're out of town. Someone who shouldn't be there. I heard a noise when I was outside, went to investigate, and caught someone running off. Could it have been another pesky reporter? Absolutely. But it felt wrong. It felt . . . sinister. I swear the hair on the back of my neck stood at attention.

I'm not that kind of person, the kind who feels evil lurking about. My time in the military drilled situational awareness into my head, but I'm still pretty optimistic about most things. And I definitely don't think the world, or anyone in it, is out to get me. At least, I didn't until after this shooting business. Add Michael's death and Rachel's unexplained absence . . . maybe it's getting to me. Maybe I'm projecting things where there's nothing.

Pulling into our driveway, the feeling returns. The doctor in me knows what it is: an adrenaline rush. Fear has stimulated my brain, bringing about a release of stress hormones. But why? I slow the car, glancing around. Nothing looks out of the ordinary. I slow to a stop several feet before the garage and turn out the lights.

"Sam? You want me to hit the opener?"

"Yeah . . . I mean, no. Just give me a minute," I stutter. "How about you stay with the children. That car following us has me spooked."

I look in the back seat. Chloe and Willie are both asleep. Good. "Maybe kind of stay quiet, and I'll see if . . . " I shrug. I'm not sure what I'm trying to say.

"Should I be nervous?" Georgia asks.

"Probably not. But stay alert just in case. I'll be back shortly to move the car into the garage and help you with the children."

Silently, I open the car door. I'm immediately blinded as the overhead light illuminates the car. Great.

I shut the door with barely a click of the lock connecting. I let out a breath, a breath I didn't realize I was holding, when the interior light turns off. I stand by the door a few moments, allowing my eyes to adjust to the darkness.

Obviously, I have no element of surprise. I've just driven into the driveway with the noise of an engine and the glare of the headlights followed by the dome light fiasco. But I'll attempt stealth anyway. I feel my hip. My pistol, or I should say, my backup pistol, is snug inside the IWB holster— exactly where it should be.

I move around the side of the garage, opening the gate. It gives a low groan. Ugh. I need to put some WD-40 on it. At least it wasn't super loud, but so much for stealth. It groans again when I shut it. I take a moment to think about how ridiculous I'm being. Georgia and I will have a good laugh about this later. Oh well, in for a penny . . .

I continue my creeping along the garage toward the back of the house. I've decided I'll take a full lap around the house, then go inside using the back door.

I'm turning the corner into the backyard when I come face to face with him. Or should I say, face to mask. His eyes widen. He takes a wild, overhanded swing. A haymaker. I'm not ready. The only reaction I can produce is raising my left hand to block the blow. But now I'm in it.

A right-hand jab he wasn't expecting to his nose, then quickly with the left, speed bag style. He's completely silent as he goes down. The screech of the patio door captures my attention—another hinge needing WD-40. In this case, I'm glad I was negligent on it. Moonlight glints off a flash of metal. A gun. I hit the ground as the shot reverberates through the night.

I do something resembling an incredibly fast crab crawl until I'm back around the corner. A second shot rings out. I have my own handgun at the ready. There's a shuffling noise—a sound I can barely make out over the ringing in my ears, my pounding heart, and my ragged breath.

I try to slow my heartbeat and silence my breathing. A slow inhale and exhale. *Calm down, Mitchell.* I repeat this process two times. One more and I'll take a look around the corner.

I'm in an awkward position at the right corner of the house, and I'm right-handed. It feels wrong, like I'll be crunched up as I try to peek around. I want to be as stable as possible, so I'm kneeling with my right knee up, attempting to create a tripod. The result: I'm even more awkward.

My plan is to lean forward quickly with only the upper part of my body, aim, and fire—hopefully before I'm fired upon. I take another deep breath, hold it, and then lean forward.

Gone. Both of them. The shuffling noise must have been the shooter helping the one I clobbered to safety.

Georgia! Could they have circled around the house, threatening my wife and children?

Chapter 18

Georgia

Sam is definitely acting weird, not at all like himself—well, not clean and sober Sam. When we were in UW together, he spent plenty of time partying. It was college, and it didn't seem to affect his classes or grades.

I did my own fair share of partying. And even more drinking on my own, in the privacy of my room. When we started dating, we partied together. No big deal. My parents both drank socially, and I figured it was the same thing.

At the time, I didn't realize my mom was no longer a social drinker. When she was injured while I was away at school, she became addicted to the painkillers. She was part of the opioid crisis, before it was declared a crisis. She mixed pills with booze. Lots of booze. I had no idea she was doing this or how bad it was. I think my dad knew she had a problem but also didn't know the degree.

As her sobriety deteriorated, she also started gambling. Some kind of speakeasy type place, completely illegal. The kind of guys who'd break your kneecaps if you didn't pay properly. She didn't see it as dangerous. Since she couldn't work, she thought this would be a good way to spend her time and earn a little money.

They didn't need the money; they were living very comfortably off Dad's machinery business and Mom's inheritance. But Mom was always looking for a bigger payday. And the excitement—I'm sure she loved the excitement.

She grew up in a fairly wealthy family. My grandpa had made some smart property investments. Land around Coeur D'Alene, Post Falls, and Sandpoint, Idaho, was fairly cheap in the sixties and seventies. He was known as a horse trader and set up some amazing deals, often helping people get out from under property they could no longer afford. He tried to make a fair arrangement, not take complete advantage of people.

Motels, hotels, single-family houses, apartment buildings, farmland, bare land suitable for dividing up into multiple parcels—he had it all, in addition to the three-hundred-acre farm he and Grandma lived on while raising their family. In the early eighties, Grandpa started selling.

He was friends with someone who said he'd heard from someone else that some big expansion plans were in the works in the area. Plans to increase tourism. Probably, if he would've held on a little longer, he could've got more money.

But selling when he did worked out fine. Unfortunately— or fortunately, depending on your perspective—Grandpa didn't live to see Coeur D'Alene become the tourist destination it is today.

Mom was the youngest of three children. She was also the only girl and definitely a bit of a princess. When she ended up pregnant, there was no question she'd be marrying my dad. Not because she wanted to; she wasn't really given a say in the matter.

She's told me many times over the years that if abortion had been legal and accessible, she would've done it. Not something you want to hear from your mom, especially when you're the one who would've been aborted. I was born in 1970, three years prior to *Roe v. Wade*, and likely the only reason I'm alive. The only reason my children are alive.

Since getting pregnant with me destroyed all of Mom's dreams, I became her proxy. I was expected to succeed. Her standards were incredibly high, and I was rarely good enough. Even though Mom made her feelings clear, Dad was always very diligent and caring toward me. So were my grandparents.

Grandpa died after a short and painful battle with cancer. I was fifteen. Grandma passed less than a year later, likely from a broken heart and exhaustion after caring for Grandpa. Even though they were extremely wealthy, they always lived frugally, so the money passed on to my uncles and mom.

Mom set enough aside to pay for my schooling through med school, and even beyond so I could have time to comfortably set up my career. She also had her own money from the inheritance to use as she wished.

Unlike my grandparents, my mom wasn't particularly frugal. Remodels to the house, new cars, and vacations were the norm. When the addictions started, she quickly blew through her remaining money.

Sam and I both did well on our MCATs. Early in our senior year, we decided our relationship was serious enough to consider attending the same medical school. I had a bit of déjà vu back to my high school boyfriend, Lyle, and our plans. But Sam and I were different.

Besides, the medical school we both wanted to attend was UW. For sports medicine, it was considered one of the best in the country. Sam was pursuing a primary care focus; UW was also perfect for this.

His Navy recruiter had tried to encourage him to specialize, but Sam had a vision of someday living a simple, possibly rural life treating his neighbors and friends. Not just treating them, but helping them to be as healthy as possible, to thrive. Partnering with Jeff is really a wonderful answer to this.

Hopefully, by the time we go back to work next Monday, things will start calming down. We'll get back to a normal routine, and we'll both be less jumpy. Less paranoid.

The *pow* of a pistol shot interrupts the silence. A second shot immediately follows. *Sam!*

My first instinct is to rush to his aid. Instead, I grab my purse and climb over the front seat into the back. "Chloe. Willie. Wake up now," I say, as calmly as I can, while I start unbuckling Willie's car seat.

"Mom?" he says drowsily.

"I need you to lie on the floor." He's unbuckled, and I'm pushing him down.

"What's going on?" Chloe asks, as I turn to undo her buckle.

"On the floor, quickly. Willie, keep your head down."

He starts to cry; Chloe quickly follows suit. They're both pressed to the floor, starting to cry softly. I retrieve my sidearm from my hip and cell phone from my handbag. There haven't been any additional shots, and nothing looks amiss.

"Shh. Try and stay silent," I say. "I need to be able to hear, to keep us safe."

Chloe sniffles, reaching for Willie, to hold his hand.

"Shh," she says to him.

"Okay," he mumbles.

I try to focus on the surroundings. What's happening? Where's Sam?

I know I should call 911. Instead, I put the phone on speaker and call Ray. It rings several times. It's late. He's probably asleep. I reach for the disconnect button as he picks up.

"Georgia?" He sounds groggy.

"Ray," I whisper, "something's wrong. There's shooting at our house. Sam . . . I don't know where he is."

"Did you call 911?" he whispers back.

"No, just you."

"I'll be right there. I'll call a unit nearby. We'll try to keep this quiet so there isn't more fodder for the media."

"Okay. Thank you."

"I'm on my way. Keep the line open."

I hear him, on what I assume is a radio, relaying information to the other unit. They're a few minutes away and will arrive before Ray.

About a minute later, there's movement. The gate to the backyard—the one Sam went through earlier—is opening. Slowly, cautiously. I see a head, low to the ground in a squat. Sam? The moon isn't providing enough light for me to be sure. I need to be ready in case it isn't him.

Chloe must have seen me tense, noticed a change in my demeanor. "Mommy?" she whispers.

"We're okay. Stay quiet, sweetie."

The person moves through the gate, still cautious. Covert. Even though the movement is awkward, it's familiar.

Sam. I'm sure it's Sam. He's okay.

"I see your dad. He's on his way to our car. I still want you to stay down and be quiet." I reach up to the overhead light and move the toggle to what I hope is the correct position so the car won't illuminate when the door is opened.

Sam's a dozen feet away, head on a swivel to take in our surroundings, as I quietly crack the door open. No light turns on. *Good.* Once he reaches the front of the car, he stoops and makes his way to me.

"You're all right?" he asks, his eyes searching my face.

"We're fine. I heard the shots but didn't see anyone until you came out. I called Ray. He's on his way, along with a patrol car or something. Said he'll try to keep it quiet."

Sam gives a grave nod. "The children?"

"We're okay, Daddy," Willie whispers. "Mommy has us on the floor. Can we get up now?"

"Not yet. Let's wait until Deputy Ray and his friends arrive."

"Okay," Willie grumps.

"I'll be there in five minutes," my phone says, causing Sam and I to jump.

"Oh, I forgot Ray's on the phone," I say quietly to Sam.

"Deputy Richardson will be there any minute. He's coming in quiet, so you won't hear any sirens, probably won't have his lights on either."

"Thank you, Ray," Sam whispers.

Chapter 19

Deputy Richardson arrives. He pulls in directly behind our SUV, motions to me, and stays in his vehicle. When Ray arrives, they carefully approach us together.

I give a quick overview of what happened. Then they check the property and the house. I know at least the one guy was inside, since he came out the patio door. *Before shooting at me.*

Once they have the area secured, we go into the house. Georgia puts the children to bed while I walk through with the deputies. Nothing seems to be missing. Richardson asks Ray if he'll finish the report. Ray agrees, then Richardson takes off.

Back in the kitchen, I ask if he'd like me to put some coffee on.

"You'd probably rather have a stiff drink," Ray says.

"I probably would. But one stiff drink is never enough for me. I'm a friend of Bill's."

"AA?"

"Yeah."

"How long you been sober?"

"Since med school, twenty-four years. Got to the point I needed to sober up or give it all up."

"Me too," Georgia says, entering the room. "Things were getting out of hand for both of us. Spending more time partying than was smart. We started AA together. My mom died a few years before. She overdosed on opioids and booze. We were afraid we might be heading down the same path."

"I'm sorry for your loss," Ray says.

"Thank you. It's hard to lose a parent like that. It wasn't just the drinking and the pills. She made lots of poor choices.

Her death brought it all to light. It also gave me a new opportunity. Did you know I was premed when Sam and I met? My mom spent the money I was to use for med school on her habits."

"Oh, I'm sorry to hear that," Ray says, shaking his head.

"I'm not." Georgia shrugs. "I never wanted to be a doctor. That was her dream for me. It was her dream for herself, and I was her surrogate. She didn't become a doctor, so I had to. With the money gone and her death, I was free. I finished my senior year of premed, married Sam, took a massage therapy course, and worked that while he went to med school.

"My dad died a couple of years later and left me the rest of their estate. This gave me enough money to go to chiropractic school. It wasn't easy. Sam and I lived apart while both doing our schooling, but it was good practice for all of his years in the Navy."

Georgia gives me a smile; I reach for her hand. We've done well together and apart for the last twenty-seven years. I've never doubted our marriage, no matter how many miles separated us.

"It's been good," I say. "Lots of flexibility with Georgia being a DC and massage therapist. It would've been hard if we were both physicians and she was trying to follow me around."

"Sounds like it worked out okay," Ray says, nodding.

"So about the coffee?" I ask.

"I wouldn't turn down a cup."

"I'll take care of it," Georgia says.

Georgia busies herself with the coffee. Ray and I sit at the breakfast bar and go over the events of the evening. My statement. It's after midnight when we finally wrap up the details.

"I should take off. First, you want an update on Rachel?"

"Anything new?" Georgia asks.

"She's still missing. And this . . . this isn't public knowledge. So you'll need to . . ."

"We won't say anything," Georgia says.

Ray nods, then says, "We found a spot of blood on the carpet. This escalated the case. Of course, the blood could've been there for weeks or even months. We just don't know. The sheriff decided it was enough to pursue. There will be a press conference tomorrow. We've already put it out on social media. There have been a few reports of various sightings, but nothing panning out."

"After tonight, I feel bad we doubted her," Georgia says.

"I understand," Ray agrees with a nod. "I'd still like to think something spooked her and she took off on her own accord. She was pretty flighty when I went over there the other night. This thing tonight, with you guys . . . I'm starting to doubt also."

"Her family?" I ask.

"Nothing. They haven't heard from her."

We visit for a few more minutes while finishing up our coffee. Ray leaves, but not before strongly suggesting we stay alert. Paparazzi isn't known to wear masks and shoot at people.

Ray and Richardson both said they'd keep it quiet, in hopes the media won't hear about it. They've arranged for even more patrols in our neighborhood. The city police were even agreeable. I suspect they aren't entirely convinced we won't sue them.

After Ray leaves, we get ready for bed. We discuss sleeping in shifts so we can keep watch. We're both still spooked. We settle for relying on the increased patrols, our alarm system, and keeping our weapons nearby.

Georgia double checks the load in her trusty 12 gauge shotgun, a gift from her dad when she was in high school. He loved duck hunting and shared this sport with her. This is her second shotgun. The first was a 20 gauge he gave her on her tenth birthday. She still has it and plans to teach our children how to shoot when they're a little older.

We don't duck hunt, although we could, but we do skeet shoot. Even though I also have a 12 gauge, I'm not nearly as proficient as Georgia. She handles it like a master.

After we moved to Wyoming, she took several tactical training courses, including one with a shotgun focus. I've taken similar courses, but she's seriously better with the shotgun than I am. My forte in advanced training is the tactical rifle. I have an AR-15 and a Mini-14, often referred to as a Ranch Rifle. I take the Mini out of the safe and make it ready.

Our handguns are in our nightstand safes. Not our preferred handguns, those are still with the police. They've yet to return them. These are pistols we've always kept by the bed. During the day, we've each been carrying a backup pistol, liberated from our main gun safe. I need to call the city police and see if there's any word on when our guns will be released.

The way things are going, I'd feel better if we had them back.

Chapter 20

Georgia

Last night was incredibly long. We tried to sleep but were both terribly jumpy. Sam finally succumbed, but around 5:00, I give it up. He's softly snoring as I creep out of bed. With his injuries, he needs the sleep.

Oh, he tries to play it off like he's fine. But I see the looks, the slight winces. He's still hurting. He's been too sore for me to do any body work, but maybe today the aches will have subsided enough for a massage to feel good. Up until now, it would've been a form of torture.

I'm still an LMT, licensed massage therapist. I kept up my Washington licensing and added additional states depending on where Sam was stationed.

Wyoming doesn't have a statewide regulation for massage therapy, neither does our county or town, though the state is working toward setting up education requirements. It's a good idea, in my opinion. Jeff and Sam want to offer massaging as part of the practice. When that happens, I'll oversee that area of the business.

The coffee is beginning to drip, filling the room with its eye-opening aroma, when I hear little feet thumping down the hallway. Willie's feet. Much more of a stomp than Chloe's soft patter.

"Good morning, little man. You're up early."

"Hi, Mommy. I woke up and wanted to see you. I smelled your coffee."

I pull him close into a hug. He smells slightly of lavender, the shampoo the children use, and a whiff of sweat. He's growing up so fast. The sweet scent of my little boy is fading.

They'll be nine in July, in the fourth grade next year. The school district has suspended classes for the rest of the year, deciding the few weeks left aren't worth trying to bring the children back. They'll advance and start fresh in the fall.

"Last night was pretty scary," he says. "I had bad dreams."

"I'm sorry about that, Willie. You know you were always safe, right?"

He shrugs. "The shooting at the school was scary too. But I knew Dad and you would stop them before they could hurt me or Chloe. I think maybe we should let me carry a gun too. That way I can help you if more bad guys come around. You know I can shoot, right, Mom?"

My sweet little boy. Eight is too young to feel he needs to be a protector.

"Thank you for offering, sweetie. Right now, I only want you to worry about being a super great eight-year-old."

"But are bad people going to keep trying to hurt us? Because if they are . . . " His face gets very hard, and he balls up his fists.

I pull him close. After a minute, he gasps, "Mom, you're smothering me."

"Oops. Sorry about that."

"It's okay. I know it's just 'cause you love me so much."

I have coffee while Willie has yogurt and fruit. Half an hour later, Chloe joins us. Then Sam comes out. I make fresh coffee for him while he goes outside. He says he wants to check the garden, but I know he's checking out the yard, the perimeter.

Our lot is oversized at two acres. This is a fairly new development and very family friendly. I wonder if anyone called in the shots last night. Ray didn't say, just assured us they'd try to keep everything quiet.

I glance out the front window. No news crews—that's good. They made them move down the road where our subdivision begins. There's a clubhouse with a large parking lot. We also have a guard station just before the clubhouse, but it wasn't manned. It is now, since the shooting.

Before they added a person, the media ignored the request to stay at the clubhouse and would park on our street. The HOA has also hired additional security and increased patrols.

The HOA president has hinted they'll be looking for a donation to help cover the additional costs. After all, it's our fault for stopping crazed killers and allowing the media to invade our quiet little neighborhood. Oh, he didn't say it quite like that, but that was the gist of what he meant.

After Sam is satisfied with our yard, eats breakfast, and has consumed an adequate amount of caffeine, he announces we're all going to the basement.

"Okay?"

"Yep. Whoever those creeps were, I think they're gone. But it's a good idea for you three to have a little self-defense training."

Great. After I just made a big deal about Willie not needing to be our protector.

Willie immediately says, "You mean, like the stranger danger class we took with Mom last year?"

"Exactly. Why don't you three show me what you learned, and we'll see if I can remember anything the Marines taught me so we can add to it."

An hour later, we're all sweaty and worn out. The children remembered a whole lot more from the stranger danger class than I did. Seems they sometimes practice together and have had several practice sessions in the few days since the shooting. Sam taught us a few simple moves to add to our repertoire.

"Let's all shower and then we'll head out to the property," he suggests.

"The property?"

"Yeah. Bring a picnic, we'll do some plinking. Maybe even wade in the creek. It's warm enough now."

"You think? We just had snow two weeks ago."

"Let's try it. Bring swimsuits, or shorts at least."

I shower first and make lunch while the rest get ready to go. When Sam's ready, he packs our Escalade, loading it with what appears to be our entire arsenal, based on the number of trips he's made. He even brings the new hunting rifles.

Sam has never hunted before, but Jeff convinced him to give it a try this year. They put in for elk and limited-quota pronghorn—called antelope by the Game and Fish—and also plan to buy a general deer tag. The draw results for the limited quota don't come out until next month. Sam's already purchased two rifles, a beautiful wooden stock 30.06 and a not nearly as attractive composite stock .338.

I used to hunt when I was young. My grandpa and dad taught me to shoot. Dad loved to hunt waterfowl. He also hunted elk and deer, but waterfowl was his passion.

I didn't put in for any draw tags with Sam and Jeff but have agreed to tag along for deer hunting. Unlike Sam, I even have my required hunter's safety card. Of course, as retired military, Sam is able to get an exemption for the card.

My new rifle is very similar to Sam's 30.06. We figured we'd buy the same caliber, for ammo reasons.

Our afternoon is enjoyable. The plinking was more than casual. Sam and I went through each weapon, shooting each one several times. I was pretty tired by the time we were done.

The children shot their .22s. Then Sam taught them on both the Mini-14 and the AR-15, along with letting them shoot my 9-millimeter pistol, the gun I'm currently using for concealed carry until my .40 caliber is returned from the police.

I know, I know. Some people would totally freak out over eight-year-olds handling such weapons. We prefer to teach them safety and to respect guns.

We're not home five minutes when Sam's cell rings—out loud. Hard to believe he doesn't have it on vibrate.

"Hey, Ray," he says.

I'm watching his face as he becomes noticeably paler.

Chapter 21

"How'd you find her?" I ask.

"Her phone came back on. We were able to GPS locate her. Found her on a piece of BLM land. She hadn't been dead long."

"How?"

"Carbon monoxide. She had a hose in the window. The car was still running. Of course, they'll do an autopsy, but I don't think things will change much."

Georgia is looking at me with wide eyes. "Hold on a second, Ray. Let me tell Georgia."

"How about I head over there? We should talk."

"Yep. See you in a few?"

"About fifteen minutes."

After I hang up, I motion for Georgia to follow me into our bedroom.

"They found Rachel?" she asks.

"They did. She . . . it seems she killed herself. Carbon monoxide."

"Not possible," she says, mimicking my own thoughts. Then she begins to cry.

I hold her tight. We both know the first instinct in suicide is denial. No one ever wants to think their friend or loved one could do such a drastic thing.

"Ray will be here shortly," I say.

"Okay. Let me pull myself together. Give me just a minute and I'll be out."

When Ray arrives, his greeting is wooden, barely acknowledging me as he walks to a lamp on the living room end table. I open my mouth to ask what he's doing. He moves his finger to his lips.

He bends over and checks the lamp shade. While doing so, he asks, "How are you and Georgia holding up?"

I give him a *what are you doing* look, but he motions me to answer.

"Uh . . . last night was long."

He goes to the second lamp and repeats the process of looking under the shade. He stands up abruptly and says in a hurried tone, "I bet it was." Then he ushers me out of the room and into the kitchen.

Weird.

Georgia is walking in from the hall. "Hey, Ray. Thanks for letting us know about Rachel."

She's struggling with her emotions, fighting hard to keep it together.

"I'm sorry I had to deliver such news."

Georgia nods. "Can I get you a drink? We have Dr Pepper, Sprite, or— "

"Sprite's fine."

We're completely silent while she gets his drink, grabs me a Dr Pepper, and makes a club soda with lime for herself. A sudden desire for something stronger than a soda washes over me.

Whiskey. I like to drink it slow with ice. Taking my time, savoring it on my tongue. Cold from the ice, then heat in my throat. A wave of warmth as it spreads down into my chest. I take a deep breath. It's been years, and I can still smell the whiskey, taste it, remember the tingle as it rushes through my body—I need a drink.

"Sam?" Georgia says.

"Huh?"

"You okay?"

I shake my head. "I need to go to a meeting."

She nods. "Me too. Found myself wishing for vodka to add to this drink. Or to drink straight. Either way would be fine right now."

Ray looks back and forth between us. "Where are the children?" he asks, running his fingers through his gray hair.

"Oh, we're not going to drink right now, Ray," Georgia says with a slight laugh. "There's just no use denying it when the urge hits. We're not leaving the kids to go on a bender."

He shakes his head. "Sorry, that's not what I was thinking. It's just really warm in here. I thought maybe we could go outside."

"Ah. The kids are in the family room. I could turn on the air if you're hot," Georgia says.

"Outside is fine."

"Sure, I'll be out in a minute. Just let me tell the kids," Georgia says.

I don't really think it's that warm inside, but I can't argue with a little fresh air. I walk toward the patio furniture.

Ray motions me to walk farther into our yard, near our small water feature, a recirculating pond with a fake rock waterfall. It's kind of cheesy, but it came with the place. We've talked about removing it, but since we plan to build a house on our property outside of town in the next few years, we leave it for the resale aspect.

Willie and Chloe race out the door. "I'll beat you to the playground!" Willie yells.

"Not this time," Chloe answers, digging in and swinging her arms. I watch as she pulls ahead, beating Willie by less than a yard. He high fives her on the win.

Georgia steps out behind them, strolling toward us. She gives me a *what's up* look. I respond with a slight shake of my head.

Very close to the waterfall, Ray says something, his voice so low I can't hear him.

"What?" Georgia asks in a whisper.

He leans toward us. "Your house is bugged."

"Those reporters!" I say, much too loudly.

Ray motions me to quiet down. "Maybe, but I don't think so. I found one in the lamp."

"What lamp?" Georgia asks with a start, color draining from her face.

"Living room," I say, "he was looking for them. I wasn't sure why— "

"I found bugs at Rachel's and Michael's also. I suspect there's more in your place. Probably cameras too."

Wringing her hands, Georgia says, "Where? The cameras, where are they?"

"Not sure. I didn't look for them. I'm just assuming based on Rachel's and Michael's homes."

"So . . . what does this mean?" she whispers. She's scared for sure but amazingly calm. I'm fuming. It's all I can do not to come completely unhinged.

I hear a whisper in the wind. *Whiskey.* I shake my head. "What do we do?"

Ray shakes his head. "Guess it's safe to say they weren't completely paranoid. And— " he takes a deep breath " — I'm starting to think their deaths were homicides."

Chapter 22

Georgia

"Homicides," I gulp.

"You really think so?" Sam asks.

Ray shrugs. "How do you guys feel about taking off for a few days? Let the dust settle a bit, go someplace nice."

"Where do you suggest?" Sam asks.

"Not sure. But don't talk about where you're actually going in your house. Call your partner. Tell him you're going someplace, like Casper, for a few days."

"I thought you said someplace nice," I mutter, while Sam says, "Casper? Why would we go there?"

"Doesn't matter. You won't go there. You'll go someplace else. Just talk about going to Casper for the listening device."

"I hate feeling like we're running away," Sam says.

I nod my agreement but know we're going anyway. We won't risk anything happening to our children.

"We'll do it," I say, while Sam nods.

"Good. Let me check your car before you go. If Michael's wreck wasn't an accident, then his car may have been tampered with."

I feel my knees go weak, as Sam tells Ray, "We just got home from our property. We took the Escalade, haven't even unloaded it yet. It seemed to be fine."

"It probably is. It's the same car you were driving last night, right? Just let me look it over, see if anything seems off. And remember, in the house, you're being listened to and possibly—*probably*—watched. You're going to Casper."

I take a long look at Ray. He's in his late fifties or early sixties, retirement age. When we first met, I noticed he's aged well and is quite fit. Today, he looks tired. "Where will we really go?"

"Doesn't matter. Anywhere you want. Don't trust your phones either. After I check your cars, how about I go and buy you a couple of burner phones?"

"You really think all of this is necessary?" I ask.

Ray pauses, then very slowly, too calmly, says, "Michael is dead. Rachel is dead. I feel like a conspiracy nut, but I have to think this is related to the school shooting. Someone shot at Sam last night. Your house is bugged . . ."

"I get it," I whisper, feeling rather sheepish.

"How long will it take you to get ready?" Sam asks me.

I shrug. "Our FEMA bags are ready now. I haven't looked at them in a while, though. The clothes are probably too small for the children. The food may be close to expired. We could grab those and add a few other things."

"Can you meet me at the rest area south of town in an hour?" Ray asks.

"Really, Ray? An hour? Doesn't that sound a little— "

"Paranoid," I interrupt Sam. "Paranoid just like Rachel and Michael. *Dead* Rachel and Michael." Suddenly, I feel the urgency—the need to go, to find someplace safe for my children.

The need for a drink comes on strong. Stress. Fear. Both make me want to drink, to relax and forget. Wherever we end up, I need to find a meeting. I need to call my sponsor. I close my eyes. *Help me, Lord. Help me to not drink today.*

"Let's get going," Sam says with a sigh.

"Act natural in the house," Ray cautions. "Don't let them know you know."

"I'm scared," I say.

"Yeah, me too," Sam agrees. "We'll be okay."

"I have a friend, of sorts," Ray says. "He can make it so it's harder for you to be found."

"I thought you said we'd take off for a few days, wait for the dust to settle," Sam says.

"You will. But while the dust is settling, he can make it so you aren't bothered."

"Like witness protection?" I ask.

"No. More like you can be . . . incognito."

"Incognito? Is that legal?" I whisper.

Ray gives an almost unperceivable shrug. "Appearing to be someone else might be safer."

"You want us to disappear?" Sam asks. "For good?"

"No, that's not what I'm saying. Just because you need to disappear for now, doesn't mean you can't reappear when we know it's safe."

"Wait a minute," I say. "Why do we need to go through your friend? Why not have the FBI or someone hide us?"

"You could," Ray agrees with a nod. "Truth is, I thought about going that route. And if that's what you prefer, we'll do it. But . . ."

"But what?" Sam asks.

"Maybe I'm the one who's paranoid now." Ray shakes his head. "I just don't think it's a good idea for anyone to know where you are. It feels like the tighter we keep the circle, the better."

"And your friend can keep this quiet?" Sam asks.

"We have . . . let's call it history."

"You've done this before?" Sam asks, wide eyed.

Ray stares at him, raising an eyebrow in response.

"How will we know when it's safe?" I ask.

"I'll get a burner phone too. We'll be able to stay in contact."

"Fine," I snap. "Let's just do it. At least the kids will be safe and we'll have a story to tell the grandkids about the time we were so paranoid we changed our names and went traipsing around the country, hiding out from . . . we don't even know who, but someone."

Sam reaches for me as I dissolve into quiet tears. Even though we're by the water, I fear they'll hear me, see me crying, and know we know. After a few moments, I say, "Let's do this."

"I hate to ask, but how are you on cash?" Ray asks. "It'll cost a little for the . . . supplies."

"How much?" Sam asks.

"He knows people. He can provide all new credentials—driver's license, social security cards, credit cards, the whole shebang. I don't think that'll be necessary. If you're okay on cash and can buy everything you need, then probably just driver's licenses and a slight change to your appearance. That'd probably be around five thousand. Then the cost of living on cash. Can you do that?"

I look at Sam. We have money in the safe, a good amount. And more in the bank.

"We have some money here. Can we go to the bank for more?" Sam asks.

"Sure. Get out enough for a vacation in Casper. That'd be totally in line."

A vacation in Casper . . . I almost laugh.

"Several thousand?" Sam asks.

"Yeah, sounds right." Ray nods.

"Will do," Sam says. "So, meet in an hour?"

"Check your watch when I leave. An hour from then. I'll text you if something changes and you need to leave sooner."

"Text what? Get out?" I ask.

"No . . . your phone may be bugged. They can mirror it and see your texts. How about . . ." Ray chews on his lip for a minute. "How about *be sure to take your fishing pole.*"

"Your text will be 'be sure to take your fishing pole' if we need to leave immediately?" Sam asks.

"Yeah. Something like that. Grab anything you can and go."

"All right," I agree.

We call Willie and Chloe over, telling them we're going on a trip and they need to start getting ready.

"A trip? Like to Disneyland?" Chloe asks.

"Even better," Sam says, with plenty of cheek in his voice. "Casper."

"Casper? Where's that?" Willie asks.

"It's in the middle of Wyoming."

Chloe makes a face. "I don't think that's better than Disneyland."

"Sure it is! We love Wyoming, remember?"

She nods but doesn't look convinced.

Willie shakes his head. "If you say so, Mom."

As soon as I walk in the door, I feel totally creeped out. They're listening to us. Watching us. Did they bug us last night? Did we come home and interrupt them? Or were they here to kill us? And if they were, why didn't they make more of an effort? Did Sam foil whatever plan they had by sneaking up on them, surprising them?

None of this makes any sense. Why target us? The obvious answer is the shooting, but why? And why Michael and Rachel?

I start in Chloe's room, packing a bag for her while Sam goes with Ray to the garage to check the cars. Will they be covert about it so, if someone *is* watching, they won't know we know?

"Do you think I should take my party dress?" Chloe asks.

"Hmm. I'm not sure you need your party dress. But we can take a dress for church. We'll probably want to find a church service while we're in Casper." I'm working hard at keeping up the ruse.

"What else will we do?"

"Maybe take a hike? There's a mountain by there. I think they have a dinosaur museum too."

"I don't like dinosaurs, that's Willie."

"I know. I was just telling you about what's there. They do river raft trips too."

"That sounds fun. My swimsuit's still in the car. I didn't get it wet in the creek since the water was only to my ankles. It's good you had Daddy build that shed there so we have a place to change our clothes when we're at the property."

"It is good. He did a nice job on it."

Another minute and I'm finished with Chloe's bag. "Here we go. I'll set this in the hall. I'm going to pack Willie's stuff."

"You need my help, Mommy?"

"You can sit with me if you'd like."

She shrugs. "Can I bring a few toys? I should get them ready if I can."

"Three things. *Small* things."

It takes only a couple of minutes to pack Willie's things. What's keeping Sam? Should I go to the garage and check? I'll pack my stuff. If he isn't back when I'm done, I'll go out.

I'm about halfway finished when he steps into the bedroom. I put on a false cheeriness. "Hey, honey. We're just about ready. It'll be good to get away for a few days."

"Y-yes. Right. It will for sure."

"I set your suitcase on the bed."

"Super. Thank you. I'm going to take a quick shower. Want to join me?"

I raise my eyebrows at him. What's he thinking . . . at a time like this?

With a mischievous grin, he says, "We'll all be in one hotel room in Casper for several days. This might be our last chance to be alone."

"Casper . . . okay. Sure."

Once we're in the shower, he pulls me close and whispers, "My car was tampered with. The Escalade is fine. Probably, since we had it last night and again today, they didn't have a chance to mess with it."

"So this is real?"

"Seems so, yes."

"We need to disappear."

"For now. To be safe. Ray will let us know when we can come home."

"Do you know where we're going?"

"No more than you do. We didn't discuss it in the garage. I set the timer on my phone. It'll take us twenty minutes to get to our meeting spot. I want to stop by the bank first and also make sure we aren't followed. Let's allow half an hour."

"Then we'd better get out of this shower and finish packing."

I'm dressed and zipping my suitcase. We were able to discreetly take our stashed money out of the safe in the closet. I considered bringing important documents like our birth certificates, but if we're disappearing, becoming someone else for a time, we won't need them. Best to just leave them in the safe.

I also tucked a travel gun-cleaning kit in my bag. We intended to clean all of the guns, then put them back in the gun safe, but never got to it. They're still in the Escalade—in a variety of travel cases—and we're taking them with us. We do add more ammo to our bags.

Our hope is there isn't a camera in our large walk-in closet, where both our personal safe and gun safe are located. We don't really want those spying on us to see us loading these things up. We hope they won't notice we never unloaded the guns from our trip out to the property.

I'm adding a few more things to my overnight bag when Sam's text indicator goes off. He's in the closet grabbing his clothes.

"Check that for me, babe?" he asks.

I swallow the lump in my throat. Not Ray. I let out a sigh of relief. I don't know the number.

My heart falls when I read it: "*Ray says don't forget your fishing pole.*"

I try to keep my voice light. "Is there good fishing in Casper? Ray says you should remember your fishing pole."

Sam chews his lip as he nods. "Good thinking. Let me cram these things in and we'll hit the road."

"Sure, honey," my voice quivers. "I'll start loading up."

My pulse is beating in my ears as I grab my suitcase and overnight bag. I juggle the suitcases sitting in the hall also.

This is real.

We're fleeing our home out of fear for our lives. They messed with our car. What if we had our babies in the car and lost control? I'm suddenly very angry. Why are we leaving? Why don't we stay here and fight? I don't want to leave my home.

I take a deep breath. First things first. We need to leave in order to even discuss this. We're bugged. They're probably watching us. Well, let them watch. I'll play along for now.

I stomp over to the garage shelf holding our FEMA bags. Living in various places, we've discovered a disaster can happen anywhere. Stationed in California, it was earthquakes and wildfires. In South Carolina and Florida, hurricanes. Here, we have blizzards and the threat of Yellowstone, the Super Volcano. Of course, if Yellowstone were to blow, I don't think our FEMA bags would be much help. And I highly doubt any place would be safe after an eruption like that.

As I'm tossing the bags in the back of the Escalade, Sam comes out with the rest of our suitcases and our children.

"Don't forget the fishing poles," I say, with as much fake cheeriness as I can muster. "I need two more minutes and I'll be ready."

I rush to the kitchen. The small cooler we took for our picnic is still on the counter. I throw things in it from the fridge—a ziplock of cold pizza from three days ago, cold chicken from two nights back, cheeses, lunch meat, yogurts. From the freezer, I add some of those little peanut butter sandwich things and a box of pizza rolls. There's a sleeve of bagels and a loaf of garlic bread. I grab a partial loaf of bread— left from today's picnic—and a pack of flour tortillas, along with a jar of peanut butter and a tub of trail mix.

If we need to disappear, we'll have food to hold us over for a bit so we aren't eating out or going into a grocery store.

I fumble with my load while trying to get out. Sam must hear the rattle of the door. He opens it for me and offers his hands. He's tense. Terribly tense. I'm reminded again how much we both need to find a meeting.

I attempt a casual smile, the smile of a woman going on a much-needed vacation. "Thank you, honey. I'm ready for our vacation."

"Me too. Glad you brought some road trip food. It's a few hours to Casper." The charade continues.

I whisper in his ear, "Is the Escalade bugged?"

He smiles and shakes his head. "Doesn't seem so," he says quietly.

"Tracker?" I mouth. I've watched plenty of television to know about such things.

He shrugs.

So . . . he doesn't know. Not good. Our ruse won't last long if there's a GPS tracker on our car. Our phones—they have GPS built into them. And our car has a built-in navigation system. Can that be used to track us?

"Hop in," he says. "Let's get this show on the road."

He starts the car. I notice the nav system doesn't automatically come on. I tap it. He gives me a wink as he calmly backs out, looking to all the world like a man taking his family on a much-needed trip. As soon as we pass the guard shack, he motions me to get out my phone.

While motioning, he talks with the kids, telling them how much fun we'll have in Casper. It takes me a minute to understand his pantomime. It takes me even longer to determine he wants me to take the battery out.

He continues conversing with the children about our trip. Once my phone is in two pieces, he hands me his phone, and I repeat the process. Only when both are apart does he speak to me.

"Thanks, Georgia. Ray told me the phones can act as a bug."

"Makes sense. Facebook always shows me things we talk about. I even have the microphone turned off in the app. It's totally creepy."

"Yeah, well, our Facebook days are on hold. No status updates until who knows when."

"I haven't updated anything since before the shooting. You?"

"Me? How often am I even on that thing?"

"How'd you turn the navigation system off?" I ask.

"Ray did it when he was checking things out."

"Are we being followed?"

"Doesn't seem so. I'm going to the bank first. Then we'll take the scenic route, just to be sure."

"You know how to spot a tail?" I ask.

"A tail? Since we're on the lam, we're using new lingo?"

"Speaking of lingo. Isn't 'on the lam' something you'd say if you were evading the police? It's not like we're Bonnie and Clyde."

"Who's Bonnie?" Chloe asks.

"You know who she is," Willie says. "She's the lady at the library, Miss Bonnie. But I don't know Clyde. Is that her husband, Mom?"

Sam and I share a smile. *They* are why we're disappearing. Even if it ends up we're ridiculous and paranoid, keeping them safe is worth it.

Chapter 23

Sam

After stopping at the bank, and probably taking out more than we should've without rousing suspicion, we take a roundabout way to meet up with Ray, driving all over Groyver and even skirting the town, taking a dirt road before heading toward the rest stop.

When we finally reach our meeting location, Ray isn't there.

"Did we miss him?" Georgia asks.

"I can't imagine we did."

"Do we need to turn our phones on?"

"Not yet."

We wait in full silence for several minutes. Every time a car drives by on the highway, we think it's him. Finally, a red Ford pickup pulls in.

"Is that Ray?" Georgia asks.

"Not sure yet." I'm wondering if I should unholster my sidearm, when I see the lights give a quick flash. "I think it's him."

Seconds later, he parks and gets out. I start to step out of our Escalade, but he motions me to stay inside. I roll down the window.

"I don't think you were followed," he says by way of greeting.

"No, I don't think so," I agree.

"I was up on the bluff— " he motions behind us " — glassing the area. Looks clear."

"And you're sure there isn't any kind of tracker on our car?" Georgia asks.

"I didn't find anything on this one. I looked in all of the likely spots, but I can't be completely sure. Which is why I found you a different vehicle."

"A different vehicle?" Georgia asks.

"Yes. It's down the river access road. Leave your car there. I'll make sure it gets back to your house. Uh, after it takes a trip to Casper. I talked to my . . . friend. He's expecting you at three o'clock tomorrow. Here's the address to meet. It's a restaurant. Take a table. He'll find you. Don't worry if he's late."

I glance at the paper. It has an address and the name of a restaurant, but no name for who we're meeting. "What's his name?"

"Call him Bob. Bob Smith."

"Okay. Sure."

"Why'd you have us leave in a hurry?" Georgia asks.

"I got spooked." He glances at the children. They're staring at him, hanging on his every word. He doesn't want to talk in front of them. Georgia catches on quickly.

"Willie, Chloe, put your headphones on. Let's put in a movie."

"I don't want to watch a movie," Chloe says.

"You know, they really just want to talk without us hearing," Willie tells her.

"Why can't we hear? Is this about our trip?" Chloe asks. Georgia gives her the mom look. The one that means business. Chloe complies with a huff and soon has her headphones on, along with a scowl on her face.

Georgia scoots as close as she can to me, and Ray quietly says, "I heard from a friend at the coroners. Rachel was high as a kite when she died."

I shrug. "That's pretty normal for a suicide to liquor or drug up. Courage by pharmaceuticals."

"Yeah, true. But he found several injection sites. Not enough to say she was an IV user. They were all fresh . . . like in the time since she's disappeared. It'd be pretty strange for someone to suddenly start using like that."

"It could happen," Georgia says. "Maybe she had other preferences, and the stress sent her over to injectables. Or maybe she had an old habit and had been clean for a while. I know the stress of the last few days . . . " Her voice fades away. She doesn't finish with, "It's been making me want to start drinking again," but I'm sure that's what she means. I feel the same way.

Exactly the same way.

"You might be right," Ray agrees. "Like I said, I got spooked and wanted to get you guys someplace safe. So go get the van. I put a few supplies in that I thought you might need. Meet up with Bob. Follow his instructions to the letter. Oh, here's the phones. I have the numbers of each. Mine is written in the note."

He hands a phone to me with a white sheet of paper taped to it that says number one followed by a phone number. He hands over the second phone, along with a phone number.

"Don't call unless you feel it's an emergency. Use the first one. If something seems off, switch to the second. If I contact you and say number two, take the battery out of number one, go to a new location—preferably several miles away—and call me on the second phone. Program the number on the paper in. Don't use the phone for anything else. Keep it on and keep it with you."

Ray hands us a car charger. "If I contact you, I'll use *salty* as a safe word. If things are bad, I'll say *gone fishing*. If that happens, dump the phone and fade away. You'll know I've been compromised. You'll then be on your own. You can get burner phones to call each other, but again, only each other. Don't use those for anything else."

I think we might be going a little over the top with all this. But instead of saying telling Ray that, I say, "Okay, Ray. Here's some money for the phones. How about the van?"

"It's a loaner. I'll get it back. Keep the supplies."

I offer him more money for the supplies. He waves it off, then thinks better of it, nodding his thanks.

"Whose is it?" Georgia asks.

"Belongs to a friend. The keys are under a rock the size of a basketball. You'll see it. Leave your keys in the same place. Better take off."

"Thank you, Ray," Georgia says, while I shake his hand.

The van is right where Ray said it'd be. It's several years old with faded paint. I half wonder if it'll get us to our meeting with Bob. We're meeting outside of Denver, in the town of Loveland. We'll need to find a map or get directions. How'd we get around before having GPS at our fingertips?

I unload our bags and everything else from the Escalade. I'm glad he got us a van so everything fits, even if it's a little rough looking. Georgia gets the children set up. There's a slight protest when Willie realizes the van doesn't have a movie player.

This is also when Chloe says, "We're not really going to Casper, are we?"

"No, sweetie," Georgia says calmly. "We're going on a different adventure."

"Do *you* know where we're going?" she asks.

"Not yet."

It takes only a few minutes to make the switch. I'm checking the Escalade to make sure we have everything, when Georgia says, "Should we leave our phones here?"

"Our possibly bugged phones? Might as well."

She nods and grabs the two phones and two batteries, setting them on the passenger's seat.

"Ready?" she asks.

"Ready."

Chapter 24

Georgia

Again, we take the scenic route. As a straight shot, we could be in Loveland the same night. We have plenty of time until we're supposed to meet Bob at 3:00 tomorrow, and we want to prevent being followed. I feel like a spy.

We spend lots of time talking with the children, giving them the age-appropriate version of what's going on. They seem a little scared but also excited for the adventure. I'm not excited. I'm only scared.

Around dark, we find a state park. Part of the supplies Ray left include a tent and blankets. The kiosk is unmanned, and there's a "Full" sign. We're exhausted and decided to go in anyway, thinking we can find someplace to park and rest. We spend the night in a day-use parking area, sleeping in the van. It's not at all comfortable.

We're on the road before daylight so a ranger doesn't ticket us. That's all we'd need. Taking our roundabout routes, we finally reach Loveland. We're an hour early and find a park for the kids to run around.

Ten minutes later, the disposable cell phone dings. A text.

"Change of venue. 3:15 in Cheyenne, Wyoming. The food is salty there, so drink lots of water."

Salty. Our safe word so we know it's from Ray, even though it's not the number we've programmed in for him. The text went on to give an address.

"What's this about?" I ask Sam.

"Safety, I guess," he says with a shrug.

We make our way to Cheyenne, arriving a little early. The address leads us to a truck stop just off I-25. We order fries and drinks while we wait.

Bob shows up at 4:00, an average looking, medium-height guy with bushy eyebrows and a prominent nose. He puts on quite the show in the restaurant, telling us how much he appreciates us meeting him and to come take a look at the RV he has for sale.

In the parking lot is a small RV, the kind with a sleeping spot over the cab. It's old and dented in spots. We walk around it as he points out the features. Then he opens it up and we go inside.

Inside, he's all business.

"All right, folks. You look like you're holding up well. Ray told me about the mess you're in. You're doing the right thing."

Sam and I nod.

"Mommy and Daddy told us what's happening," Chloe says. "Mostly. Are you the man who's going to help us . . . "

"Disappear," Willie finishes for her.

"Yep. That's me. So here's the plan. I have new driver's licenses for you, Mom and Dad. I didn't get you two driver's licenses, thought you might be a little short to reach the car pedals."

Both children laugh, then Willie says, "Dad's teaching me how to drive. I can probably do it pretty soon."

"Is that right, sport?"

"So we just have new licenses and that's it?" I ask.

"Not completely it. You need to change your looks to match the photo. The children need a disguise also, so I've included things for them. This here will be your home for the next several days. We're going to a house up the road so you can take care of your hair and stuff. While you're doing that, I'll finish getting things ready. Ray said you have bug-out bags?"

I give him a strange look. Sam says, "Our FEMA bags."

"Okay." Bob shrugs. "You'll have a car to tow behind. Once you get where you're going, unhook the car and put your bags in there, and also anything else you don't want to be without. It'll become your bug-out car, an emergency escape vehicle."

"Where will we camp?" I ask.

"I have a spot reserved for you starting tomorrow night, down in southern Colorado. Tonight, find a spot along the way. In a few days, no more than a week, a friend will show up at the campground. He'll set you up on the next leg of your journey."

"Okay," Sam says. "Ray said we'd pay you."

"Yep, three thousand for the IDs. The RV is a loaner. The car . . . well, let's say fifteen hundred for it. You good with that?" He doesn't wait for us to answer. "When my friend meets you, a thousand for him . . . for his trouble. He'll give you everything you need for the next steps."

Sam gives him the money. Bob gives us the address to the apartment, not far from where we are now, in a middle-class neighborhood. The apartment is almost completely void of furniture. There's a table in the kitchen with several reusable shopping bags on it—hair dye, clothing, a hair clipper set, and more. Our disguise kits.

I'm now June Jefferson. June is my middle name. Bob said he would've liked to keep my first name since it's easier to answer to a name you know, but Georgia is too distinct. And Georgia and Sam together . . . not good. Bob said the children should go by their middle names also. Chloe is now Abigail; Willie is Oliver.

They think it's great fun to have new names. They're even more excited when we tell them they'll be getting new hair.

Both have gone from a deep brown to light brown, almost blond. I'm now a dark reddish blond. The color on the box showed a much lighter golden blond, but my auburn hair didn't cooperate. It looks fine, especially with the green nonprescription contacts.

Sam is bald, his white scalp like a beanie, with piercing blue eyes thanks to his contact lens. Bob included an assortment of hats, sunglasses, and nonprescription glasses in our disguise kit. Sam will definitely need a hat in public until he can get a little sun on his reflective head.

Once we're ready, we go back outside. The RV, parked on the street, now has a small economy car attached to a dolly. The car is in about the same shape as the RV. Fifteen hundred may have been too much for it.

We put the children's car seats in the RV and then let them explore inside while we get our final instructions from Bob.

"You guys cleaned up right fine," he jokes. "Seems the clothes fit okay. You'll look like vacationers, spending your time on the road. Ray said you lived in California for a time, so I switched out the tags to show you're from there. Pick a place you're familiar with as your home base. There's another set of plates in the bottom drawer in the kitchen. Switch to those once you get to the campground."

"All right," Sam says. "Mind if I ask how you and Ray know each other?"

Bob gives a small smile. "Not sure that's really my story to tell."

"It just seems . . . Ray is with the law and you . . . "

"Are on the wrong side of the law? I guess it may seem that way. I look at it as providing a service."

We're all quiet for a few moments, then he pulls out another phone. "This is your number three. The programmed number will reach Ray. Give me the number one. It's done."

"Why is that?" Sam asks.

"The text. We're following a one-and-done protocol. Use number two now, same protocol. Keep it on and charged. Contact Ray only in an absolute emergency. He'll contact you if needed or when it's safe to go home. If you use number two, dispose of it and switch to number three."

"How do we reach you?" I ask.

"You don't. When you leave here, we're done. My friend will see you within the week for further instructions." Bob gives us a long, hard look. Then he softly says, "Ray busted me for making fake IDs. This was years ago when he was with the Colorado State Patrol, before he wanted the quiet life in Wyoming." Bob gives a laugh.

"Hasn't really been that quiet, and now with you guys . . . anyway, I got a slap on the wrist. That was back when things were different, not all computerized like now. I've kept up with the times. A few years ago, Ray found me again. He needed my help. His high school girlfriend needed to escape an abusive situation, and he asked if I could make her a new identity.

"I thought it might be a trap he was setting up. I'd branched out a bit from fake IDs to . . . well, more. Turned out to be legit, she needed help. Over the years, Ray has come to me with other women in similar situations. He's almost running an underground railroad for abused women."

"Really? That's wonderful," I say, thinking of Tawny Ridgely and one of her charities—Bell House, a women's shelter.

"It is. And I've probably said more than I should've about it. But you need to know this isn't our first rodeo. You might think of me as a criminal, and I am." He waggles his eyebrows. "But not all of what I do is for other criminals. We've done some good things, helped some people who really needed it."

"You do that pro bono?" Sam asks.

"Not your concern, friend. Time for you to hit the road. Find a small town with a mom-and-pop grocery store. Get enough food and supplies for a week. I don't want you out and about once you get to the campground. Only one of you goes in the store. Take one of the children if you wish, not both.

"You guys will be all over the news soon. They'll be looking for a family of four. Don't socialize. Don't make friends at the campground. Keep to yourselves. Here's the address to the campground. Half a block down, the cul-de-sac ends. The turnaround is plenty generous to get the RV out of here. Forget you met me."

With that, he takes off walking, leaving the van we were driving.

Sam shrugs, then says, "Guess we better get going."

We make the cul-de-sac turn and head out of the neighborhood. There's no sign of Bob.

Chapter 25

Sam

We took Interstate 80 heading toward Laramie, stopping at a gas station to top off the tank and buy a map of Colorado. It was well after midnight before we finally reach our chosen destination—a campground in the Grand Mesa Colorado Forest.

Willie had the sofa, Chloe had the converted dinette, and Georgia and I slept above the cab. It's been hard for me to remember to refer to them by their new names. Chloe has reminded me several times to call her Abigail.

The next day, we're outside of Alamosa at a good-sized private campground. Bob reserved us a spot far from the office.

We stopped in a couple of stores along the way to get the supplies we felt we'd need. We tried to stick to smaller stores, ones we hoped wouldn't have video surveillance, and took turns going inside.

One of the stores was nothing more than a convenience store attached to a restaurant and bar. The options there were rather limited. The hardest part was when I went to pay, which was at the bar. The small bottle of Jack sitting by my left arm seemed to keep inching closer. I started to negotiate with myself; *just one bottle, and I'll make it last. A sip or two each day to take the edge off.*

I admit, I'm angry. Bitter even. Part of me wants to go home and make a stand. I hate that these people, whoever they may be, forced me to flee my home, my life. I've fought hard for the life we have. There was a time when my path didn't look too promising.

Drinking and partying in college wasn't a big deal, or so I thought. When I tried to continue the party lifestyle into medical school, I was almost booted out. I couldn't keep up, and my grades suffered. One of my professors took me aside, told me to get it together and then directed me toward Alcoholics Anonymous.

I started AA on a wet and windy day in January. Georgia supported me but didn't think she had a drinking problem. Two weeks later, after a blackout-drunk session, she also started visiting the Rooms.

When talking with Ray, I'd told him I was sober twenty-four years. That's not exactly true. I've had a few relapses following deployments and other stressful times. It's been nine years, eight months, and four days since my last drink. The day Georgia told me she was pregnant.

She also gave me a final ultimatum: return to sobriety or she'd raise the baby on her own. Baby. At that time, we had no idea we were expecting twins.

My sponsor wouldn't have been impressed that I lied to Ray. Why'd I lie? Maybe because I didn't want Ray to think less of me? Not good. Definitely not good. My disease has made me an excellent liar.

It's so easy for me to think about how I deserve a drink, to justify it. After all, my life is in shambles. A sip or two would at least ease the stress a bit. While alcoholism is a disease, drinking is a choice. I can choose not to drink. AA works well for me and has given me so much more.

In AA we talk about a higher power—God, as we know Him. AA brought me to wanting to learn about God, which brought me to His son, Jesus.

Once I became a follower of Christ, a Christian, I started looking for an AA alternative. There are a few Christian-based Twelve-Step Programs. These tend to be pretty good, but not as readily available as AA. And for me to stay sober, meetings are essential.

And now we're hiding out. I can't even go to a meeting for fear of being discovered. Georgia and I have rarely attended meetings together. It's just not comfortable for us.

Many times, AA and Al-Anon will meet at the same time, in the same building but in different rooms. We've found this works well for us, switching off who goes to AA and who goes to Al-Anon. After all, we fit the criteria for both; we're both drunks, and we both have problems with someone else's drinking.

We're also both children of addicts. Her mom died directly from her disease by overdosing. My dad died driving drunk. Thankfully, the only life he took was his own.

These last few days, since we can't go to meetings, we're attempting our own thing—a meeting of just the two of us. It's not the same, but it's helping. I'm not waking up in the middle of the night thinking about how I can sneak out for a drink . . . or ten. We're also reading our Bible much more consistently. I'm thankful Georgia thought to pack a Bible.

Somehow, I managed to get out of that bar without the bottle of Jack. Now more than ever, I need my wits about me. And who am I kidding, a sip or two . . . yeah, not my style. While I love to savor whiskey, it never stops with a sip or two. And I can't risk my family's safety for the momentary release a bottle would bring.

The first night in the campground, we talked for hours, finally having time to process these newest events. Being forced from our home and the indications Michael and Rachel were murdered—while it makes little sense, it all has to go back to the school shooting.

The three of us foiled their plans and possibly saw something we shouldn't have seen. The dead boy. Apparent self-inflicted gunshot wound to the temple. Not carrying a gun. Was it supposed to look like he was the only shooter and then killed himself instead of being arrested?

We've unhooked the car and set it up with our FEMA bags, camping supplies from Ray, and guns. We're now on our third day at the campground. We've followed Bob's instructions and have kept to ourselves. When getting supplies, Georgia picked up games and books, along with a portable DVD player and several movies. She even bought a couple of CDs for the RV dash player. She bought quite a bit of food. Some of it we're keeping in the car, shelf-stable stuff we can eat cold or heat with a small stove, part of the supplies from Ray.

It's around lunchtime on Thursday. "Getting hungry?" Georgia asks.

"I am!" Willie cries.

"Me too," Chloe agrees.

"I could eat," I say. "Let me— "

We all jump as the text indicator on phone number two goes off. Heart pounding, I grab it.

"*Gone fishing, caught a whopper.*"

Georgia is looking at me with wide eyes. I nod, barely keeping my composure. "Time to go."

Worry written on her face, she grabs her purse. I take the battery out of phone two. We'll dispose of it down the road.

"Let's go, kids," Georgia says.

"Bad men coming?" Willie asks.

"Not sure. But we have to leave now." I hand the keys to Georgia. "You drive." I take my pistol out, to have it at the ready.

"Shotgun?" Georgia asks.

"Too big, too noticeable. Nice and slow through the park. We're just heading out to sight see."

She gives me a *duh* look.

Our sedate pace is maddening. Every part of me wants to have her floor it. Good thing we didn't. At the office is an Alamosa County Sheriff patrol car. His door is open and one foot is on the ground. Georgia mutters under her breath. I watch in the side-view mirror as he finishes getting out of his car. He doesn't look our way.

We reach the paved county road. "Which way?" Georgia asks.

"Turn right." I pull out the map. "Okay. Looks like there's a road a few miles ahead, on the right. Let's take it."

Five hours and many backroads later, we're in Chama, New Mexico.

"Find a park or something, somewhere the children can get out for a bit. I'm calling Ray."

"You'll use our last call," Georgia cautions.

"Yep. I know."

While the children play, Georgia and I make the call. Choosing not to use the speaker function, we scrunch together to hear. He answers on the second ring.

"You okay?" he asks.

"Seem to be. What happened?"

"She recognized you, or rather, your tattoo—the lady in the office—when you bought ice last night. She called it in to the hotline this morning. Seems she went back and forth on whether it was really you or not, but finally convinced herself. Randolph took the call, told me about it, right after he called the sheriff department down there to check you out. You need to cover that tattoo."

My tattoo, staff of Asclepius, a healing symbol, on my calf. I was wearing shorts yesterday. I didn't even think of it. Stupid. Stupid.

"How'd she know about my tattoo?"

"Part of the description. They got a pretty detailed one of you from your recent hospital visit."

"Well, that's convenient," Georgia huffs.

"Sorry, honey." I pull her close. "I didn't even think about it."

Tears well up in her eyes as she nods. "Me neither." Georgia quickly composes herself. "Ray, so, the sheriff at the office?"

"Yep. He was there for you. They're sitting on the place, waiting for you to return. My concern isn't the sheriff department, of course."

"Your concern is, whoever is behind the shooting, may have inside information," I say. "Someone on the payroll somewhere?"

"That's about the size of it," Ray agrees.

"Where do we go?" Georgia asks.

"Rawlins, Wyoming. Hampton Inn. There will be a package for Kara Mathews. Have Georgia go in for it. Be there the day after tomorrow at 4:00 p.m."

"It'll be safe?" I ask.

"I hope so," Ray says with a sigh.

"I pray so," Georgia says.

"Yes, that too," Ray agrees.

We disconnect and I pull Georgia into my arms. We spend several minutes holding each other. Then I whisper a prayer, petitioning for Our Father to keep us safe, to keep our children safe. We reluctantly end our embrace after the *Amen.*

"Time to go," I call to the children with as much enthusiasm as I can muster.

We cross back over into Colorado, heading to San Juan National Forest. We find a forest service road to set up camp. Georgia and the children sleep in the tent. We have blankets but no mattress pads. We cut branches off pine trees and cover them with a tarp, compliments of Ray, to provide a little cushion. The children love it.

Georgia and I will take turns sleeping, keeping one of us on watch. She'll sleep first since she's been driving all day. Watch is from the passenger's seat of the car, where the overly zealous mosquitos can be locked out.

At 3:00 a.m., we swap places. The pine branch bed leaves much to be desired, and the tent is too short for me to lay in anything but the fetal position. The next day we take our time leaving, then drive through Durango. We make a much-needed stop at a small outdoor store where Georgia buys four incredibly over-priced backpacker's blowup mattresses and a second tent.

The tent is small but still takes up serious space in our compact car. At least I'll be able to stretch out. We spend the night on the Grand Mesa. The mattress and tent are both wonderful.

We pull into the Hampton Inn in Rawlins at 3:45. Right on time.

Chapter 26

Georgia

I'm nervous. When I go into the hotel for the package, will cops be waiting for me? Will they put me in handcuffs and drag me out? Will Sam have time to escape with our children, or will they get them also? Will our children be remanded to family services?

No, of course not. We're not criminals. The bigger threat is that we'll be found by the people who killed Michael and Rachel. We scan the parking lot, first by driving around the hotel a couple of times, then the lot itself. Everything looks normal. Sam parks the car, positioned so we can leave in a hurry.

We purchased two disposable phones and Bluetooth earbuds so we can stay in contact, just as Bob suggested when we met with him in Cheyenne.

"You ready?" Sam asks.

No.

I take a deep breath and nod.

He dials my new phone—my spy phone. I answer and he mutes his end.

"Walk a few steps away. Let's make sure I can hear you."

"Testing, testing, I'm just suggesting . . . "

I turn and look at him. He gives me a thumbs up and a weak smile. My heart is pounding. I try to move with confidence—head up, strong stride. I'm wearing my disguise of a floppy hat and regular glasses, the ones Bob gave us with plain lenses. The contacts still feel weird in my eyes. And I need a shower. A really long, hot shower. We've been using baby wipes, but . . . ugh. Maybe Ray has a room waiting for us.

"How may I help you today?" the incredibly cheery, incredibly blond desk clerk asks.

"Hi there." I attempt a smile. Act normal. "A friend was leaving a package for me. Kara. Kara Mathews."

"Oh, sure. Let me get it."

She steps to an office or something, returning shortly.

"Can I see your ID?" she asks sweetly, not realizing my heart is dropping to the bottom of my stomach.

"Oh, I left my purse in the car." True story. I lift my hand, showing only my phone.

"You want to run and get it?" She smiles then looks down at the box. "Oh! Never mind. There's a note on the box that ID isn't needed." She pushes the box across the counter toward me. "Here you go, Ms. Mathews."

"Thank you." This time my smile is completely genuine.

I walk calmly back to the car.

Into my spy phone earbud, Sam says, "Way to go, babe."

When I'm in the car, I say, "Go somewhere else so we can open this up."

"How about the mini-mart we saw on one of our drive-bys?"

"Perfect," I say, disconnecting my spy phone.

At the mini-mart, Sam pulls out his pocketknife. Not the one he killed the guy with; the cops still have that one and both of our pistols. He bought a new knife. I hated losing my pistol. My backup is fine, but that one . . . I sigh.

Inside the box are two cell phones, labeled one and two. Guess we're starting our count over. There's also a set of keys and an envelope with driver's licenses, along with a note saying, "Call #1." The phone has a number saved to it.

"Do this here?" I ask.

He looks in the backseat. The children are asleep. "Might as well," he says.

"Speaker?"

"Okay, yeah."

I make the call.

"Hello, Kara, darling," a female answers—a familiar sounding female. "Give me just a minute to step outside."

Speaking to someone else, she says, "Can I sit outside? The table by the water? Perfect. A white wine, please."

I wait until she says, "Okay. Go ahead."

The gentle sounds of a waterfall, cascading over the rocks, similar to the one at our home . . . what used to be our home, is now in the background. I'm suddenly taken back to my yard, the expanse of green grass, the children laughing from the playset, the gentle song of a meadowlark—

"Are you there?"

"Tawny?" I ask.

Sam has a completely dumbfounded look on his face.

She gives a small laugh. "I thought old *Bob*— " she says his name like she's doing air quotes " —might have mentioned me. You didn't think Ray was helping all those women on his own, did you? You know about my charity."

I do know about her women's shelter, but I had no idea about this. "So . . . the stuff he told us, you allowed him to tell us those things?"

"Right. I kind of thought you might put it all together. Doesn't matter."

"Does Jeff know?" Sam asks.

"Of course. He helps with the funding."

Sam and I exchange a look, while Tawny continues with, "Your situation has escalated. Ray is being followed, and his house was broken in to. He's been bugged. There's a good chance our place has been too. I left for my trip early. I left the day after you. I'm still in the US but heading to Spain in a few days. Jeff doesn't know we're helping you. He never knows the details of who we help. It's better that way, and especially in this case. Besides, you know how Jeff can be a bit of a gossip and always— "

"Tawny," Sam says, trying to reel her back to our situation.

"Oh, yes. Sorry. So here's the thing, we can give you some final tools, but you'll have to go it alone—disappear fully and completely."

I gasp.

"It doesn't have to be forever," she says. "Just for now."

"Where should we go?" Sam asks.

"Don't leave the US. You'll get caught at the border unless you could sneak across. It's not worth the risk. Find someplace remote. We have a new car for you at the TA truck stop there in Rawlins, gray Suburban. Use the ID in the box, but then switch to what's under the seat when you get where you're going. Stay hidden and stay sharp. Don't use the last phone. Keep it at the ready, as you have been."

"Are we . . . are we going to be okay?" I can't help but ask.

She sighs. "We don't know who it is, who's doing this. We usually protect people from abusive spouses not . . . whoever this is. Bob has a little more knowledge of these kinds of . . . entities. He thinks the reach is probably pretty wide. The package in the Suburban will give you a deep cover. He's worked his magic to make sure you can pass scrutiny, everything you need to start a new life. How are you on cash?"

Sam and I share another look.

"Not good. I don't know if we'll have enough to— "

"Understood," Tawny interrupts. "I'll pay Bob's newest bill. You'll need every penny to set up a new life. You can pay me back after this mess is over. Be sure to read your resume, especially your skills so you can get a job."

"Um . . . "

"Not your doctor skills. Blue collar stuff."

"Blue collar, no problem," Sam says.

I look at him and he shrugs. He reaches out and touches my cheek, wiping away a tear. I didn't even realize I was crying.

"Okay. Bob gave you a generic work history. It'll be in the package, probably things like waitressing and custodial. Can you do those things?"

"Absolutely," Sam says. "We'll be able to do whatever is necessary."

"All right, then. I'll be home mid-June. I hope this is all settled and we can see each other then. Leave the keys in the car you're driving."

"Sounds good, Tawny," Sam says.

"Take care, my friends."

I say goodbye but the phone clicks off. She already hung up.

Sam shuts it off and removes the battery. He steps out and throws it in the mini-mart garbage can by the door.

We're on our own.

Chapter 27

Sam

Georgia cries all the way to the TA truck stop. Not that it's very far, only a few blocks. When we pull in, she immediately sees the Suburban. It's old, like 1990 something. We take a lap. Nothing seems out of the ordinary . . . other than our whole lives are a mess.

It takes a few minutes to transfer everything to the old Suburban. The children wake up, and we get them situated. Georgia sets up the portable DVD player for them, giving them each headphones.

"I guess you two want to talk in private," Chloe huffs.

Georgia smiles and says, "Just for a little bit. We need to make new plans."

"Adult plans," Willie says.

"Right. As soon as we know what's happening, what we're doing, we'll talk with you about it," Georgia answers.

"Why can't you let us help with the plans?" Chloe asks with a pout.

Georgia bites her lip; she's having trouble with her emotions.

Chloe sees it and softens her demeanor. "Okay, Mommy. We'll watch the movie and then you can tell us after you and Dad have things planned."

"Thank you, Chloe. Have I ever told you how grown up you're becoming?"

Chloe shrugs.

"Me too," Willie says. "We're pretty much the same age, you know."

"I'm still older," Chloe says, sticking her tongue out at him. So much for being grown up.

The Suburban engine fires up. It sounds great. I test the blinkers, lights, and everything. All seem to work fine. I turn on the air conditioner, hoping it also works. I fiddle with the radio. It won't turn on. Guess we can live without a radio.

"Where to?" I ask, pulling out of the parking lot.

"How about west," Georgia says.

"On I-80? Why not? Then we can decide what to do, where to go."

"This beast has a tow hitch, right? Can we tow a trailer?" she asks.

"Maybe. A small one, anyway."

"I was thinking about my cousin Sandy. Remember how excited she was about us moving to Wyoming?"

"I guess. Because you guys vacationed here as children, right?"

"Yes, more on the west side, though, closer to Yellowstone. And she's gone there several times since. She had a boyfriend she met on a trip to Florida. They made arrangements to meet up for a vacation in the little town we used to visit. They rented a cabin in Bakerville, that's the little town we visited thirty-five years ago. He liked it so much, he bought property while they were there and planned to build a cabin. He died when a plane he was piloting crashed . . . you remember this? It was only a few years ago. The twins were toddlers."

I shrug. "It sounds familiar. Sandy said we should buy the property his estate was selling for our own vacation retreat, right?"

"Exactly."

"So . . . is it still for sale?"

"It was last summer. She mentioned it again when we were chatting on Facebook. She even sent me a link to the listing. I showed it to you. Remember?"

Not really, but I don't want to admit this. Her memory is amazing. Mine . . . not so much.

"It's been for sale for five years? Seems like a long time."

"I told her that last summer, along with asking what's wrong with it."

"She said the area had a lot on the market for a while and things weren't selling. It was picking up, but the property is kind of unique."

"What does that mean?"

"Limited building spots. The driveway is long and unmaintained, plus it'd cost a mint to get power back there. Power currently ends at the start of the drive. There's a water well already drilled and set up to use with a generator. That was her big selling point to me, said we could use solar since it's just a vacation home. Another selling point, it's eighty acres and connects to national forest. There's a working farm of some sort on one side and a few other houses around, but it's very private."

"If it's so great, why didn't she buy it?"

"Her husband hates it there. Hates Bakerville and doesn't want her old boyfriend's property."

"Can't say I blame him," I mutter.

"So . . . what do you think?"

I pause. "What do I think? So you'd like to drive to . . . "

"Bakerville."

"Mm-hmm. Wherever that is. And then we'll just squat on land that's owned by a dead guy's estate. At least, we think it's owned by a dead guy's estate. Can you even find the place?"

"Bakerville should be on a map. It's north of Prospect, which is north of Cody."

"Okay. But can you find the property?"

She's very quiet, staring off into space. Finally, she says, "I think so. Pretty close, anyway. I know we'll go by the community center. It was highlighted on the directions. Then the road makes a Y, take the next road. I think the road Y's again and becomes gravel. Then . . . I'm not so sure. But maybe it'll come back to me when we get there."

I sigh. "So you want to buy a camp trailer to live in while we squat on the land? And if it's no longer for sale?"

"The beauty of Bakerville is it's on the edge of national forest. There are several access roads suitable for pulling a trailer. We can stay awhile. Regroup. Maybe even just wait this out."

"I don't know, Georgia."

"You have a better idea?"

With a shake of my head and a large sigh, I say, "No, I guess not."

"Oh, and you should start calling me June. We're currently Sam and June Wilcox. And our final IDs for when we reach Bakerville are . . . "

She's working to get the envelope out of the glove box and opened.

"Oh! Tawny wasn't kidding. We have credit cards, birth certificate, and social security numbers. Nice to meet you, Mr. Sam Copeland. You used to . . . " She stops and laughs. "You've had an interesting work history. Dump truck driver, clerk in a hardware store, most recently we were caretakers on a chicken farm in Arkansas. Ick."

"What? No janitor job?"

"You should be so lucky."

"What about you?"

"I drove a paper route, worked in a coffee shop, and helped wrangle chickens. Have you even been to Arkansas?"

"I have. What town?"

"Judsonia. We left because the chicken farm is for sale."

"Nope. Don't know where that is. I've been to Fayetteville."

"So . . . maybe we need to find a library? Research our cover story?"

"Yeah. How do we get to Bakerville?"

Chapter 28

Bakerville is just as beautiful as I remember. Finding the property took some doing, but we did it. An old, weathered *for sale* sign was at the bottom of the long mess of a driveway.

We stayed on the interstate until we reached Green River, then headed north toward Riverton, sleeping in the Suburban at a wide spot off the road—another roundabout route, in hopes of ensuring we weren't followed.

In Riverton, we shopped for a camp trailer. We found one in the local *Nickel Ad* and bought it using our throw away ID. It was super easy. The guy's wife was a notary. We have forty-five days to put new tags on it . . . but I'm not sure if we actually will.

It's nice. There's a small bedroom at the front and bunk beds in the back next to the tiny bathroom. A slide out dinette and slide out couch really open up the space. It included a Honda generator. Sam bought a second generator to use for the well pump.

We visited the library in Riverton to research Arkansas and the other details in our history, making copies so we could study them in-depth later.

We stopped again in Cody and Prospect for more research and copies, thinking it'd be good to not make all the copies at the same place. Keep them guessing!

We bought lumber and stocked up on groceries too. Sam wants to build a railing for Willie . . . I mean, *Oliver's* bed so he doesn't fall off the top bunk. He bought plywood, too, for building a doghouse.

Yeah, a doghouse, for another *Nickel Ad* find. When Sam first mentioned getting a dog, I envisioned Cujo—one who'd rip a bad guy's throat out if they tried to hurt us. Nope. He found us a yappy little thing.

I have no idea what it is, other than scraggly and older. The person thinks she's around four or five. She went crazy when we pulled up—we could hear her from the street where we parked—and even crazier when we knocked. Sam declared her perfect.

Her uncreative name is Gizmo. It fits.

Sam also bought a roll of three-foot wire and posts to make a fenced area.

"Poor Gizmo won't have to sleep outside, will she?" Chloe, now called Abigail, whined.

"Nope. She's sleeping inside. But she'll need fresh air. If we're working outside, she can be in her dog run."

"Like when we're planting the garden?" Willie/Oliver asked.

"Exactly," Sam said.

Another purchase was 2" x 12' boards to make garden boxes, and lots of soil. We bought lettuce and radish seeds, quick producers, so we can have fresh produce for the children. The garden store had a few old seed potatoes. We added squash plants, both summer and winter varieties, tall and leggy, way past prime planting. The nursery lady said they should be okay and gave us a deal. I pray we'll be home before they mature.

Getting into the property took some doing. The road was terrible from the start and washed out in a low area.

"This is good, in some ways," Sam said. "It'll keep people out."

"Yeah, but can we get in?"

"We'll be fine going in and out once we don't have the trailer. This thing is a tank. But for now . . . " He fully stopped, looking at the washed-out area. "Let me do some work on it."

He pulled out a shovel, part of the garden store purchases, and evened out the area. I asked if I could help, but he waved me off.

After fifteen minutes or so, it looked better, good enough we were able to cross.

We've been here just over six weeks. *Six weeks.* We've yet to hear from Ray or Tawny on our special phone. Cell phones don't work very well here. The reception is terrible. So we keep it off most of the time, hiking up to the top of the hill every morning and evening to check it, assuming we'll get a text if there's anything important.

We've switched to our final identities: the Copeland family.

Sam's growing his hair out, and we're dying it a sandy blond. My hair is almost jet black and obviously dyed, like I'm making a statement. I think I'll pick up one of those burgundy washes to soften it a bit, maybe help it look a little less harsh.

The children are very blond. We're not using the tinted contact lenses, just sticking with wearing glasses, either the nonprescription ones or sunglasses.

Truly, the only one needing a disguise right now is me. I'm the only one that goes to town. Sam and the children stay here day in and day out. I've asked Sam if it's getting to him, if he's handling it okay. He thought about it a bit before telling me he's doing great, much better than when he was in the Navy, even better than when we lived in Groyver.

We've planted our garden, built Gizmo's run and doghouse, and continued to work with the children on shooting their rifles, plus have taught them how to clean the guns—an important part. Every day we practice self-defense.

The trailer is fine. It gets hot during the day, so we stay outside. There's no shade of any sort on the property. What I wouldn't give for a tree or two. I've made a few nerve-racking trips into Prospect and nearby Wesley, where I was sure I was going to be recognized. On one trip I bought a shade thing used for camping. It's also surrounded by netting to keep the flies away. Thankfully, we don't have mosquitos. It's too dry.

We quickly discovered the generators burn too much fuel. We discussed our options and decided on solar. Not having the internet at our fingertips is terrible, so we discussed our plans, then I'd drive into Wesley or Prospect to use a computer at the library.

After surfing the net and finding what we discussed, I called Sam—on my spy phone, the ones we use only to call each other. He was expecting my call, so he and the children were on the high hill behind our trailer.

Turns out, we needed more info, so I had to buy another phone and call the company. It was the right thing to do. I wouldn't have ordered everything we needed, and the lady gave me some tips on other things to buy.

Then I bought a couple of prepaid credit cards and set up a mailbox at a mailbox store, where USPS, UPS, and FedEx all can be delivered. What a process!

The system costs way more than I wanted to spend, but we need water. There was no getting around it. The helpful lady gave us a discount, and she even included a small separate system to provide a little power for our trailer. Because of shipping hassles, we didn't get batteries for either system.

The trailer does have a built-in battery system, now charged by either the generator or connecting it to the Suburban and running the vehicle. Sam thinks he can hook it up to the solar panels to store the solar energy for nighttime use. We'll see.

The solar system for the well pump will fill a cistern— easily purchased at a local feed store—when the sun is shining, so we'll always have water. The cistern sits on blocks, lifting it slightly off the ground so we can remove the water. We fill the holding tank in the trailer so we have running water inside. Sam is working toward figuring out how to connect it so it's less labor-intensive.

We don't know what we'll do if we're still here in the winter. With the cistern above ground, will it freeze?

The lady at the solar company suggested several other things for living fully off the grid. Some things she could provide, others needed to be ordered from other sources, and a few bought locally. The final cost was crazy. After I got everything ordered, I trashed the phone.

I stocked us up even better on groceries during that trip, enough to last until fall, I think. I've always tried to keep a well-stocked pantry. Now, it seems smart to keep as much on hand as we can. Every time I go into town, I'm taking a chance of being recognized. Also, with the terrible road in and out, a good rain or snowstorm and we'll be stuck for days. Possibly weeks.

Along with food, I bought clothes and other supplies. Even totes and shelves to organize things. It was a full-day trip. And it was utterly exhausting.

Sam bought a small utility trailer we saw on our first day in Bakerville. It was on the side of the road with a *for sale* sign.

On my massive shopping day, I towed it and brought lumber and other items back to build a shed for storing our supplies. After the solar system came in, I used it to haul the cistern home.

These past six weeks have been very busy. Building up a place to live from bare ground takes a lot of work. Even if we're squatters on the land, we want to make it comfortable, usable.

Once this whole debacle is over and we can return to our real lives as Dr. Sam, Dr. Georgia, Chloe, and Willie Mitchell, we'll buy this land, giving them whatever their asking price is, and then some, for the privilege of using it. And we'll come clean about squatting on it.

We plan to build a little vacation cabin. Living here these several weeks has convinced us that this is one of the most beautiful places on earth. It's a perfect vacation spot.

Even though we have so much work to do each day, we've still tried to enjoy the area, hiking up into the national forest or driving to a secluded spot on the river. We've even found a few small lakes in the forest.

We're not becoming a part of the community, of course. We're trying to be very stealthy about who sees us. Buying the trailer from the lady down the road was probably a mistake in itself—one we realized afterward. She did say she was selling it so she could move to South Carolina or somewhere, so maybe it wasn't too big of a deal.

Besides her, we've seen our next-door neighbors, a black man and woman who've waved at us a few times while they were riding their four-wheelers.

Today is Sunday. Since we can't go to church, for fear of being recognized, we hold our own services. We've been doing an almost-daily service of sorts with Bible reading, singing, and discussion. Sundays, we beef it up a bit.

This has been wonderful, not only for our Christian walk but for sobriety. Like Sam, who told me he's doing better than when we lived in Groyver, I can honestly say my desire for drinking is diminishing each day we're here. Even though we fear for our lives, our entire reason for being here, things are so calm and serene. We don't have the day-to-day stressors, those things we tend to blow up in our minds and think only a drink will alleviate.

Of course, when I was drinking, I didn't need a specific reason to drink. I'd drink to relax. I'd drink to celebrate. I'd drink to mourn. *Oh, a B on a paper? Better booze it up.* I'd drink to fit in. Whatever the reason, I could drink. I *would* drink. I even loved the flavor.

I can't tell you how many times I wished I could just be like a regular person, enjoying one fancy drink when out to dinner. After we started AA and I was sober for a while, I thought maybe I'd made a mistake. Maybe I wasn't really an alcoholic, a drunk.

Sam was deployed and I went out with some girlfriends. They were drinking while I sipped a Sprite. I finally said, "Why not?" and ordered a Cosmopolitan. Which soon became three Cosmos. Those three turned into a four-day bender, along with the realization I'm truly an alcoholic, just like my mom.

I refuse to pass this on to my children. Yes, there's a genetic link to alcoholism, and those genetics can lead to a predisposition to alcohol. Chloe and Willie know of our struggles. We speak to them openly and honestly about the effects alcohol has had on our lives.

After our morning church service, we work on the storage shed we're building. We're down to the final pieces. It looks pretty amazing and will be even better once it's painted. Sam is on top of the shed with the radio on. The reception is terrible at ground level, but on top of the hill or on the roof, it tries to come in. The news announcement brings me to my knees.

Chapter 29

Sam

"More news from Groyver, Wyoming, the site of last month's school massacre. Sheriff Deputy Ray Sandoval has been killed in the line of duty. Details are still forthcoming on the actual nature of the event."

"Sam!" Georgia gasps and collapses in tears. "They got him."

Are we jumping to conclusions? No. Occam's razor: *the simplest solution tends to be the right solution.* They killed him. It's the most likely explanation.

I quickly climb down from the roof and drop to my knees, pulling Georgia close, holding her as she cries. My own eyes are filling up.

After many minutes, Georgia whispers, "What does this mean for us?"

I sigh. "I'm not sure anything changes. Not really, anyway, other than we know they haven't given up. We haven't talked to Ray since that day in New Mexico. He has no idea where we are. Tawny told us to disappear. She doesn't know where we are either. No one does. We stay here, wait it out."

"The final phone?"

I'm sure I have a panicked look. We haven't kept it on. There isn't service here, at least not reliable service. The first few days, it'd sing out and we thought we were getting a message. Instead, there was a notification saying *leaving service area* or *entering service area.*

Now we keep it off, and every morning and evening we climb the big hill at the back of the property and turn it on to check for messages. I take it out of my pocket, fumbling madly as I try to remove the cover and rip out the battery.

Hopefully Ray didn't have this number where they could find it. Hopefully they haven't already pinged us.

"Are we okay? Do we need to leave?" Georgia shudders.

"I don't know," I answer honestly.

"So how does that work?" Before I can respond, Georgia continues, "They have the number. They get a court order to see if the number pings off any cell towers. How accurate is that? Where is the cell tower even at? We leave it off most of the time. Does that help?"

"I don't know. They can find them on TV when it's off, as long as the battery is still in."

"We're not on TV," she says softly.

"Yeah. I don't really know. Remember how Ray said they found Rachel because her phone came on? Maybe, since ours is off, we're fine. Yeah, we should be fine." I hope I sound convincing.

Georgia gives me a long look and then a slow, sad nod. "We're probably safe."

We spend the rest of the day grieving. Grieving and wondering if they—whoever they may be—can find us by the final burner phone.

The next day we start on an escape hatch of sorts, a plan to go up and over our mountain and into the forest. We set up a cache of supplies—canned food, the tent Ray gave us, blankets, and a few other things. We use two plastic totes secured with duct tape, bury them in the national forest, and then cover them with rocks.

We hope the cache will be bear proof. We saw a grizzly bear a few days ago, heading up the mountainside. It was well away from our place, but still . . .

We also make a plan for a notification system, something so we can know if someone's coming up our driveway or crossing our fence line. As we start putting these things together, we both wonder why we hadn't done these things before. Not very smart on our part.

After breakfast on Monday, Georgia goes into town to find a remote alarm system and motion detector lights.

She was able to find some of what we needed. The rest she ordered using the library computer. Everything should arrive by Friday. She also bought another handgun, a 9-millimeter she found on a local *for sale* corkboard. Got to love a small Wyoming town!

She met the lady at the McDonald's. After Georgia checked it out and agreed to the purchase, they chatted for a few minutes. The lady's husband died, and she was getting rid of most of his guns.

Georgia asked a few questions, which eventually led to how much for all of them. The deal was too good to pass up and included ammo to go along with each gun: a 9-millimeter, a .357 revolver, a .22 rifle, a 270 rifle, a 30.30 Winchester, and a 12 gauge shotgun. Bingo!

Georgia bought more ammo at a retail store and rounded out the shopping trip with more supplies—a combination of dry goods, canned items, and some dehydrated meals to add to our FEMA bags and to make a second cache. Our second tent, more blankets, and some of the weapons will also go in the new cache.

We continue to fortify our place, clean and sight in the new rifles, and work on self-defense.

Chapter 30

Georgia

It's Friday morning. I'm going to town to pick up the items I ordered, plus additional supplies from a new list we put together. I can't believe the excellent deal I found for the guns the other day. When we set up our first cache, we put the handguns we used to keep in our nightstand in the container, so the two additional pistols were a great find.

Today, I'm buying some PVC pipe so we can make a cache for the new rifles and shotgun. Yeah, yeah, I know. Paranoid. But our paranoia is keeping us alive.

My first stop is the mailbox store. The lady in the store, who I've met several times now, hugs me when I walk in.

"Oh, June," she cries, catching me totally off guard. "This is so terrible. It's like 9/11 all over again."

Confusion paints my face.

"You haven't heard?"

"No, what happened?"

"Terrorists. They crashed airplanes and then blew up the airports when the firemen and ambulances arrived. So many people were killed. Some reports say it might be double the losses of 9/11."

"Oh no! I . . . I haven't heard." It's all I can do not to start crying.

"Would you like to go into my back room and watch the coverage? I've been going back every little bit to see if there's anything new."

"Would you mind? Just for a minute? The radio in my car doesn't work, and I don't want to wait until I get home."

I spend fifteen minutes catching up on what I've missed. It happened last night. Sam was reading to the children by the light of an oil lamp when the first crash happened.

Within a matter of minutes, four planes were down. All flights were grounded, but not soon enough. A fifth plane crashed. Then they started blowing up airports, with multiple bombs at each location. No one is claiming responsibility.

"Thank you for the use of the television," I say, walking out to the clerk.

"Terrible, just terrible," she says. "I'm so glad we're so isolated here. Wesley is such a safe place. We're so small, no one would think of attacking us."

I nod my agreement. It takes me three trips to get everything to the car. Using the spy phone, I try Sam. Straight to voicemail, which we haven't set up. He isn't expecting me to call, so he wouldn't have been up on the hilltop waiting. I send a text, asking him to call me. Maybe the text will go through.

Do the plane crashes change anything for us? I don't think they do. As tragic as the crashes and following explosions are, it doesn't directly affect us. I'm still June Copeland, an out-of-work chicken farmer, wearing fake glasses, with jet-black hair and considering a burgundy wash. We're still hiding out, trying to keep our children safe, trying to survive.

I finish my shopping without hearing back from Sam. I get everything on the list we agreed to, plus add a few more things—several more things, really. Sure, it's unlikely the attacks will directly affect us, but I can't shake the feeling that I should do something . . . something more. Just in case.

I'm halfway home when my phone rings.

Chapter 31

Sam

"Sam!" Georgia cries when answering. "Give me a second, I need to pull over."

My heart is pounding. It has been since I received her text. All it said was, "*Call me as soon as you get this.*" It only came through a few minutes ago when the children and I hiked over near the edge of the property. We practically sprinted to the top of the hill so I could call her.

"Are you okay?" I ask, not waiting for her to pull over.

"I'm fine. We're fine."

I take a deep breath and nod to the kids, then give them a thumbs up. She scared the daylights out of me. I thought someone recognized her. I thought . . .

"Sam, I'm here now. There was an attack last night. A terrorist attack."

"What? Where?"

"Here, in the US. Five planes were shot down, then they blew up the airports. Not near us but in the United States."

"Oh . . . " I know this is big. I know I should be upset. But all I can think is she's fine. We're fine. *Thank you, Jesus.*

"Sam?"

"I'm here. I thought . . . when I got your text, I was scared. It's terrible about the attacks, but I'm glad you're okay. Are you coming home soon?"

"Sorry. I didn't mean to scare you. I wanted to talk with you to see if you thought the terrorist attacks change anything—for us, I mean."

"Do you think they do? I mean, it's awful. I'm sure lots of people have died, but as far as us . . . I don't know. Unless Wyoming was directly affected, or Bakerville specifically, I can't see how it'll affect us."

"My thoughts too. I did buy a few extra things that weren't on our list, and all of our supplies arrived, so I shouldn't have to go back into town any time soon. We'll be set for weeks."

"Sounds good. C'mon home. We'll climb the hill and listen to the radio when you get here, see what the latest is."

"Okay, I'll be there in about twenty minutes or so. I love you."

After I disconnect, Willie asks, "What happened, Dad?"

"I'm not really sure. There was some kind of . . ." I pause to choose my words. "Something happened last night, and several airplanes crashed."

"How'd they crash?" he asks.

"I'm not sure. It sounds like someone, some people, may have done it on purpose."

"Why?" Chloe asks.

I shake my head. "I don't know. Let's walk back down to the trailer. We'll wait for your mom to get home, and after we unload everything, we'll see what we can find out. But I want you to know, whatever happened, we're safe. We're fine right here."

Neither child looks like they believe me.

Once Georgia is home and we get the newest purchases put away, we climb the hill with our little radio. Other than what she told me on the phone, I learn little more.

Oh, sure, I do learn which flights were brought down and in which cities. I learn the president gave a great speech according to some, and a terrible speech according to others. We both agree it has zero direct effect on us.

We shut the radio off, hike down the hill, and go about our day. The new supplies are just what we need to set up the security system. I have it ready by dinnertime. After we eat, we trek back up the hill to check in on the latest news.

"*. . . bridges were targeted by handheld surface-to-surface missiles, with devastating results. As of now, we have confirmed reports of forty-eight bridges affected, with* varying degrees of damage. We will provide the list of these bridges after I have finished speaking with you."

"The president?" Georgia asks. "Is he talking about new attacks?"

"It sounds like it," I answer.

". . . today's attacks, we are closing or limiting access to other bridges across the nation that we have determined to be likely targets. Last night, our nation came under attack with the deliberate crash of five airplanes while attempting to land. This was followed by the detonation of multiple explosives at and very near each airport experiencing a crash.

"Today, we continue to see evil with the destruction of our bridges. The loss of innocent life is staggering. Immediately following last night's attacks, I implemented our emergency response plans. Our emergency teams are working at all five cities that were attacked. These cities are Queens, New York; Miami, Florida; Los Angeles, California; Chicago, Illinois; and DFW Airport in Texas.

"With the bridge disasters, we are distributing teams as we can to all affected areas to assist the local fire and rescue departments. I ask for your cooperation, as citizens, to help where you can and to obey all requests from your local government. Let us come together during this time of tragedy and show those who oppose our very way of life that we cannot be broken by their cowardly acts. We will find those responsible and bring them to justice. None of us will forget these times, but we will persevere. God bless each of you. God bless America."

"What's going on?" Georgia asks.

I shrug, as the radio announcer says, *"That was a replay of today's earlier address from the president. After last night's airplane crashes and subsequent explosions, today, we have once again been targeted. There have not been any bridges in Wyoming affected, but a Denver bridge was hit."*

The local announcer goes on to recite a list of affected bridges. Many are well-known landmarks. She finishes her announcement with, *"We will continue to update you as more information becomes available."*

"Oh no," Georgia says. "I don't understand how two things like this could happen in two days. It'd have to be a coordinated attack, right?"

"I can't imagine anything else making sense."

"There aren't any bridges around here, right?" Willie asks. "The lady on the radio said nothing was— "

"Affected," Chloe interrupts. "Nothing affected in Wyoming. That means they didn't blow anything up around here, right?"

They're both wide eyed. Georgia shares their look.

"We're okay, guys," I say. "Nothing changes for us."

"But there's a river on the way here. We had to go over a bridge to get here. Mom, didn't you drive over the bridge today?" Willie asks.

"I don't think that bridge is going to be a problem," Georgia says, taking a deep breath, trying to calm herself for the children. "It's a very small bridge. The ones mentioned are very big bridges."

"Have you been on any of them?" Chloe asks.

I nod. Georgia's eyes fill with tears as she says, "Yes, several of them. They're all very far away from here."

"Okay, guys. How about we go back down to the trailer and play a game?"

We leave the radio off until Chloe and Willie are asleep. Then Georgia and I take it outside and climb up on the roof of the shed, keeping the volume very low. There's music playing. We take that as a good sign. After several songs, the announcer comes on, a man this time.

"We've received several updates about the traffic problems following the bridge explosions earlier today. While things are still fine in Prospector County, many of the towns along the southern Wyoming section of I-25 and I-80 have been severely impacted.

"People are fleeing Denver, where the Speer Boulevard Bridge was destroyed earlier today, and converging on

Cheyenne, Laramie, and even towns farther from Denver. Denver area television and radio stations are encouraging people to stay in their homes and to heed advice from their local officials, but it doesn't seem to be helping.

"Even with the clogged interstates, more people are still attempting to escape Denver. We know Denver is not the only town facing a mass exodus. Every city with a bridge attacked is in a similar situation. Highways and interstates across the United States are clogged with people seeking safety. We'll keep you posted on this latest information."

"I don't understand why people would leave their homes," Georgia says.

"Same reason we did, I guess. Fear for our safety. Fear for our children's safety."

"I guess."

Chapter 32

Georgia

Even though Sam and I talked well into the night, I'm up before the sun. After listening to the radio, Sam doesn't think the bridge attacks and mass exodus from Denver, as the announcer put it, will be an issue for us here.

I disagree. Clogged roads will cause major transportation issues. What if the truck that brings groceries to the SuperMart in Prospect can't get through? Sure, we have a fair amount of food. More than a fair amount, quite a lot. But I feel a burning need for more. And not just food but other supplies too.

One of the things we've done in the weeks we've been here is build up our medical supplies. Back home, in Groyver, we had an impressive medical kit. Being married to a doctor has its perks. We carried a small trauma kit in the Escalade, which is still with us, but the rest of our supplies we've been working to replenish.

Even though we're both alcoholics, neither of us have had an issue with narcotics—we could, for sure, but we've decided keeping a few narcotics in the FEMA bags made sense. I creatively hid five hydrocodone in my bag and five in Sam's bag.

What we didn't have were things like suture kits, topical analgesics, local anesthetics, antibiotics, and several other things we've made a point of keeping on hand. The internet is an amazing thing, and I was able to order many of the items needed without any kind of prescription.

For antibiotics, I visited a feed store in Wesley. I could buy injectable penicillin for livestock over the counter. Of course, it states it's not for human use, but my doctor husband said it'll work if we need it. At the SuperMart in Prospect, I bought oral fish antibiotics. I've ordered suture kits, casting supplies, and other equipment off the internet. Sam jokes he could do surgery if needed.

He may find it funny, but I find it essential. We're hiding out in this little enclave of Bakerville, an hour from the nearest hospital. What if something happened to Chloe or Willie? Having my own on-site doctor is wonderful. Having the supplies my doctor husband might need is imperative.

Today, I want to drive into Prospect. I want to buy more food, more medical supplies, toiletries, clothing—especially for the children—gasoline, and anything else I can think of.

Chapter 33

Sam

"Georgia, for once, *just once*, could you do what I ask?"

"Seriously, Sam? What's up with you? Aren't we usually a team?"

"Then act like it. We don't need more supplies. You've bought plenty of food and things on the numerous trips you've made to town since we got here. I have an idea. How about you let me go to town this time? How about that?"

"Sure, Sam. You can if you want. The only reason I've been going is I thought we agreed it was safer. If you've changed your mind, go ahead and go." She gives me a strange look, then whispers, "Sam? What's going on?"

We're sitting outside, watching the sunrise while the children are still sleeping.

"What? Nothing. Nothing's going on."

She stares at me. I know the look. I glare back, trying to stare her down. A single tear escapes down her cheek. The tear causes me to crumble. I know what she's thinking.

"I'm not drinking." I sigh. "I want to be, God knows how much I want a drink. Me going to town is not a good idea."

"You're acting the way you used to act."

"Yeah." I run my fingers through my hair. It's still short, crew cut short, but at least I'm no longer bald. I know exactly what Georgia's referring to. When my drinking hit its high point, or low point depending on perspective, I had a serious personality shift. Where I used to be the fun, life of the party drinker, as a full-blown drunk I was mean—almost sinister.

Hostile.

The hostility was what brought me to the realization I needed help. Drinking was no longer working for me. Whiskey was no longer my friend. *Whiskey.*

Now here I am, snapping at my wife, acting all guilty. No, I haven't been drinking.

Only because there's no booze here.

I stand up and step slightly away.

Georgia watches me as I begin to pace.

I did briefly consider the rubbing alcohol she purchased as part of our medical supplies. Isopropyl alcohol isn't anything like whiskey. It's not even made the same. Isopropyl alcohol is made in a factory. It's pure chemical, essentially a solvent. But it'll get you drunk for sure.

Too drunk.

People die from drinking rubbing alcohol. My doctor brain knows this.

My drunkard brain still stared at the bottle, wondering if a little sip might give me a nice buzz without leading to my death. Just a slight release, a break from my new identity and the terrible disasters happening around the US. Normal people drink when they want a break. Maybe, after being sober so many years, I might be normal.

Normal. Yeah, fat chance.

No, not worth the risk. Rubbing alcohol is metabolized quickly, meaning the effects would slam into my nervous system. That little sip—and who am I kidding, it wouldn't be one little sip—would be incredibly potent. Dangerously potent.

"I haven't been drinking," I say. Then, in a barely audible whisper, I add, "But I want to. It's starting to consume me."

Georgia's face softens. She stands up and walks over to me. More than anyone, she knows how I feel. Being married to a drunk isn't easy. Being a drunk yourself isn't easy. Right now, I'm a dry drunk. Not drinking but behaving like a drunk.

"All right. What's causing this stinking thinking?" she asks quietly.

"You name it. Feeling sorry for myself started it. As much as I've loved this time we've had together, I miss my practice.

I miss . . . being Dr. Mitchell. It's been brewing for a few weeks, hanging in the back of my mind."

She starts to say something, but I hold up my hand to have her wait. "I know. I did say I was doing fine. And when you asked, I was. But since then . . . " I shake my head.

"And now, with the attacks, I'm feeling useless. If we weren't in hiding, I'd be volunteering, going where I was needed to help. But instead, we're here, in the middle of nowhere, pretending to be out-of-work chicken farmers. Chicken farmers, Georgia!"

A slight smile crosses her face. "Yeah. I guess that'd be a bit of a blow to the old ego."

Ego, is that what this is about? My ego is hurt? No, that's stupid. "It's not about ego. It's about being where I'm needed. Don't you think they're hurting for doctors?"

"Yes, I do think they're hurting for doctors. I also think, even if we weren't in hiding, fearing for our lives, for the lives of our children, you still wouldn't be able to help."

Ouch. Did I forget we're hiding from murderers? I choose to ignore that for the moment. "Why wouldn't I be able to help? Would you stop me?"

"Really, Sam? Stop you? I've always been behind you— no, not behind you, beside you. Right next to you, even when you were on the other side of the world. I was always with you, Sam."

Her tears return. I pull her close as my own eyes fill up. She's absolutely right. She's always been with me.

In a voice so quiet I strain to hear, she says, "How would you get there, where they need doctors? Planes were grounded on Thursday. Interstates near the cities with the bridge explosions are parking lots. How is help going to reach the people who need it?"

I step slightly back from our embrace to look in her face. She's right. Transportation would be a challenge. "Surely FEMA and the National Guard have something figured out."

"Maybe so, Sam. Or maybe they will have in a day or two. Either way, you're needed here. And we both know

your issue is you, not what's going on anywhere but here."
She points to my head.

Minutes pass with us simply looking at each other. Finally, I say, "My name is Sam. I'm an alcoholic. It's been nine years, nine months, two weeks, and six days since my last drink."

"Hello, Sam," Georgia says with a small smile.

Chapter 34

Georgia

After having our two-person AA meeting, Sam relents. He agrees another trip to town isn't a bad idea. He does bring up an interesting point. He asks if my own ego, my grandiose thoughts, might be part of my need to buy more stuff, my need to control the situation.

I've been stocking us up on food and supplies since we arrived in Bakerville in case we found ourselves unable to go into town for whatever reason—mainly in case it becomes too dangerous. Is that trying to control the situation? Most likely. But it also seems terribly smart. Not just the grandiose thoughts of a recovering alcoholic.

With these attacks, who knows what could happen? If interstates are clogged, will the grocery trucks be able to restock? Can fuel trucks bring more gas? Will Prospect and Wesley be affected?

I take the trailer so I can buy more building supplies too. We've decided, in case we're still here when winter hits, our little trailer home could use a mudroom.

As always, it's a slow go, weaving my way down our long, bumpy driveway. The washed-out area, which Sam has to work on every time it rains, isn't too bad today. Also on my list: gravel so we can try to build up the base. We'd love to order a load of gravel, but we worry about the possibility of being discovered as squatters. Living on the lam certainly has its challenges.

Where our driveway meets the main road—a slightly improved, well-graveled version of our pothole riddled goat trail—are two other driveways. The driveway to the north belongs to the couple we often see on their quads; at least, we think it does. We haven't met them, just waved from a distance.

Their place sits back from the road. From here, I can't see their house at all. From a butte above our trailer, we can catch a glimpse of their place, nestled in a slight cove between a pair of small hills. From the looks of it, they've done some nice things. We spied a garden and several trees, even a lush swatch of grass.

As lovely as their place looks, it pales in comparison to the second driveway. This one heads to the south. The property is nothing short of amazing. Closest to the road are lots of tall, native sagebrush. Goats and/or some sort of long-horned cattle are often in the field. We don't think they're a Texas Longhorn, but maybe a crossbreed. Farther back from the road, near the farmhouse and other buildings, is a virtual oasis.

While the house on the north is lovely with the trees and grass, this place takes it to a whole other level! Trees, vines, multiple gardens, and so much more—it's absolutely swoon worthy. Definitely unexpected in the high desert of Wyoming. I can't even imagine the amount of time and money they must spend to make everything so green.

They do seem to have a crew helping them. There are always people going in and out. Today, there's considerably more activity at the oasis farm. Looks like maybe they're planning a party.

I stifle a sigh, wondering if we'll ever be able to participate in a neighborhood party again. Or will we always have to keep our heads down and keep to ourselves? What kind of life will that be for Chloe and Willie?

Today, the larger town of Prospect is my destination—specifically the SuperMart and building supply store. And probably a few other places before I head home. My focus is preparing us for winter. Yeah, preparing for winter in June. Sounds pretty dumb.

Everything goes well. Finding winter items is the challenge I expected it to be; the regular retail stores only has summer things available. A stuffed-to-the-gills pawn shop has several things. The pawn shop owner directs me to a used clothing store operated by his church, and I find many items there. A sporting goods store has boots and a few other things on clearance. Overall, I do pretty well.

By the time I'm loaded up with food, supplies, lumber, and other things, I'm exhausted. I decide we're having a treat today. Pizza. It won't be piping hot by the time I get it home, but it'll still be delicious.

It's just past the lunch rush so not terribly busy. I order and wait at a booth, sipping a soda. An older couple in a nearby booth keep stealing glances at me. I try to be totally casual, adjusting my ball cap so it sits a little lower, shading my face. I take another sip of soda. *Beer. I wish it was a beer.*

They finish and start to leave before my to-go order arrives. Walking by, the man says, "You having a good day?"

I smile and attempt a fake southern accent. "Yes, thanks."

"Have we met somewhere?" he asks, scratching the stubble on his chin.

"Now, Harve," the woman says, touching his arm, "I told you not to bother the lady."

"Sorry, Miss. You just look so familiar." He shrugs.

I'm nervous, sure I'm recognized, but try to be nonchalant. I give my hair a little flip, scrunch up my nose, and drawl, "Ya ever been to Macon, Georgia?"

"Macon? Nope. Don't even know where that is."

"Oh. I don't know then. I'm just passing through, staying with some friends, then heading back home . . . you know, once the traffic troubles are fixed."

"Of course. Terrible thing." He nods. "Hope you have a safe trip."

I watch them walk out. Nothing seems amiss as they get in their car and drive away. I'm still concerned. Did they recognize me? Will they report me to the sheriff or FBI or whoever is in charge of looking for us? The news on us had died down, but then when Ray was killed, it revved back up.

I really need that beer. Instead, I practice some antianxiety breathing exercises.

Finally, my pizzas are ready. I take a look out the window again before leaving. Everything in the parking lot looks fine. Even so, I take a long drive around Prospect and then into Wesley—an extra thirty plus miles—before finally heading to our Bakerville hideout.

Our usually private, quiet gravel road going to our mess of a driveway is terribly busy. I meet over a dozen cars. The party at the oasis house must have broken up. The line of people leaving their driveway is substantial. I shudder a bit, thinking of how many people have witnessed me driving into the property—the property we don't own but are using as our residence. I'm mentally kicking myself for not pulling over and waiting for the pack of cars to diminish.

I make eye contact with a man in a large Dodge pickup. He gives me a small smile and a slight wave, common in Bakerville. I respond with a slight head bob, hoping my disguise is acceptable.

The pizza is a congealed mess of cheese by the time I reach the trailer. Even so, Sam and our children still welcome it. They're happy to see me also, but mostly the pizza. I turn on the oven to give the food a quick warm-up.

"How was town?" Sam asks.

"Sad. Lots of people are in a fog over what's happening."

"Sounds about right."

"How are you?" I ask, searching his face.

He makes a bit of a face, scrunching up his lips and wrinkling his nose. His forehead follows suit, along with a slight shrug of the left shoulder. "You know, I'm pretty good. I'm not going to lie and tell you I didn't think about drinking today, but I think we both know it's a rare day when the thought of a drink doesn't cross my mind."

"And mine. We're alcoholics, it's to be expected. The question is— "

"I know. I didn't drink today, so today was a success."

I reach for him. Like him, I didn't drink today. Sure, I thought about it. I even had the perfect opportunity. But I didn't drink.

One of our adages, "Live one day at a time," is a reminder to focus on the moment. I don't have to worry about the things I did when I was drinking, the things I did yesterday, even the argument Sam and I got into this morning. I also don't have to worry about tomorrow—will I drink tomorrow? It's not something I need to focus on when living in the moment.

With our new life, the days kind of blend together. It's been wonderful, but it's also harder to live in the moment, to live one day at a time. I totally get Sam feeling useless while he's not practicing medicine. If I dwell on it, I'll feel the same way. But living in the moment, in the here and now, we're doing what's necessary: protecting our children.

Before I can share my thoughts with Sam, our alarm system dings. The children, both sitting at the table starting on their slices, look up with wide eyes.

"It's the driveway," Sam announces, while looking at the alert sensors nestled in a plastic cleaning caddy on the counter.

"Chloe, Willie, shoes?" I ask.

Chloe is slipping on a pair of crocs while Willie points to his tennis-shoe-clad feet. He grabs Gizmo's leash and attaches it to her collar.

"Anything happen in town?" Sam asks.

"No . . . Oh. An older couple asked if they knew me."

He frowns.

"It was nothing. I wasn't followed. I made sure," I say quickly, as I move the children toward the door. "I even went through Wesley instead of coming straight home. Oh, and there's a party or something at the house with the gardens."

"A party?"

"Yeah, I saw them setting up on my way out, then everyone was leaving when I came back."

"So . . . they saw you?"

"Of course they saw me. Let's just go. We'll talk later." I hope this is true. "Ready?" I ask everyone. I make eye contact with Chloe. She's silently crying. Willie reaches out and grabs her hand.

"It might be nothing, right?" Willie asks, a sheen of tears filling his eyes.

"Absolutely. It probably is," I say.

Sam grabs the caddy holding the alert sensors off the counter, then peers out the window. "Looks clear. Let me go out the door first, then you guys know what to do."

We've parked the trailer so the entrance is facing the hillside behind us, giving us—we hope—a way to exit without being seen. The new alarm system is set up in various locations around the property. In theory, no one should be able to sneak up on us.

Sam is slow and cautious as he exits. We've practiced this several times in the past few days. Even before we had the alarm system fully set up, we practiced exiting and our next steps. Not that we really know what we're doing. Sam's military training—even what he had with the Marines—didn't really cover this, not terribly in-depth anyway. The things we're doing, we mainly learned from watching TV.

"All clear. See you soon," Sam says. He gives each of the children a quick kiss, then touches my hand. "We'll be fine."

I nod. "Let's go."

Chloe, Willie, Gizmo, and I run behind the trailer. There's a natural ditch we've designated as part of our escape route. This ditch will provide cover and concealment, plus a runway, of sorts, to get away. We can take it and, as the saying goes, head for the hills.

If it turns out this is something rather than nothing, the children and I will probably be on our own. Sam will do what he has to do to buy us the time we need to retreat to safety. I suck in a breath. *Please, Lord, let this be nothing.*

Sam races to the shed. After Ray was killed, we attached a box to the side of the outbuilding that holds his Mini Ranch Rifle with a large-capacity magazine on a sling, a tactical bag with additional filled magazines, more ammo, a small pair of binoculars, and his beefed-up FEMA bag. A little additional research at one of the libraries showed me just how much stuff we'd been missing.

We've put a ladder against the shed and built rungs into the roof. These rungs are how we were able to hang out on the roof and listen to the radio the other night. This vantage point also provides a great view of our driveway and down the gravel access road, along with a panorama of everything but the hill behind the house. In the last few days, in addition to the rungs on the roof, we've given the shed additional advantages, such as being reinforced along the sides with concrete blocks.

One of the things I picked up today were sandbags, thinking they could add a little more security to the shed and our cover ditch. Now I wonder if we'll get a chance to pursue this new project.

"Climb down," I say to Chloe as calmly as I can muster. Willie is still holding her hand, giving her balance as she climbs into the ditch. The children have created something like stairs out of the slightly compacted soil, making it easier to access the trench.

Similar to the box by the shed, I have my own cache. Mine holds a shotgun, not my favorite one given to me by my dad, but one we didn't mind leaving in a space not fully protected from the elements. The homemade wooden box, while semi-weathertight, isn't worth the risk of my heirloom.

Instead, we've stashed Sam's 12 gauge. Also in the box are the FEMA bags for each of the children and me, plus ammo and a walkie-talkie.

I fumble with the padlock, messing up the code on the first try. I take a deep breath and try again. Success.

"Papa Bear," I say into the radio.

"I'm here, Mama Bear. Give me a minute."

Chloe and Willie are scrunched down in the ditch, completely out of sight, hugging each other and Gizmo. Willie looks up, meeting my eyes. I give him a small smile.

"Mama Bear, I think we're okay," Sam says over the radio. "There's a herd of deer making their way up the side of the hill. I think they set off the alarm. They might have been spooked by one of the cars on the road. There's still quite a parade leaving that house."

"That's good, right, Mom?" Willie asks, while pulling Chloe even closer.

"That's good," I agree.

"Let's wait a few more minutes, just to be sure," Sam says through the radio.

Chapter 35

Sam

Yesterday's scare has me wondering how I can prevent the local wildlife from setting off our detectors. After thinking about it, I'm slightly surprised it hasn't happened before today. I'm sure, in the time we've had our system set up, other deer, antelope, and possibly elk have passed by. Maybe even a bear, either grizzly or black. We know they're around, having seen scat nearby and a bear in the distance.

Our alerts aren't anything fancy, just simple wireless systems in a combination of brands. We purchased the basic systems locally, now set up so they capture a large swath of fence line. Each of the motion detectors send a chime to its corresponding battery-operated receiver.

We've made a control center, of sorts, in a plastic cleaning caddy. This caddy goes outside with me when I'm working around the place or, as in the case yesterday, if the alerts go off. Next to the rungs on the roof of the shed, I've added a small plywood platform to hold the caddy. When we're in the trailer, it sits on the counter by the door. I've labeled each of the receivers so we can tell where the threat is originating.

The driveway sensor is the most advanced of all and has only been set up for a few days. Because our driveway is so long, we ordered an alert with a half-mile range. It's a pretty slick solar-powered system, with four sensors set on four different receiver chimes. This lets us have a sensor at the entrance to the driveway and at various intervals.

The intervals are helpful in case someone was to come in overland. The land we're using—squatting on, as Georgia keeps reminding me—isn't fenced in the driveway area, making it easy to walk in. We talked about adding fencing to

"

this section, but with the rocks in the ground, a simple post-hole digger isn't going to cut it. We'd need a power auger.

Checking out the sensor at the driveway entrance, I see the ground is well trampled with deer tracks. I didn't notice any tracks when I put the sensor out. Maybe they usually use a different route to get into the wilderness area behind us, but with the party yesterday, they created an alternate trail to avoid the people.

I deliberate for several minutes on changing the focus of the sensor, finally deciding its current angle is the best choice. We originally wanted to set up a camera option, instead of just a driveway alert, but finding something that'd work in our situation—without any internet or Wi-Fi—didn't happen.

Georgia did bring home some information on systems that are self-contained, not needing an internet connection, but the need for continual electrical power prevented us from jumping on those. Now, I'm seriously wishing we had a camera down here.

Maybe Georgia should spend a little more time at the library tomorrow to see if there are any options for a camera at the bottom of the driveway that'd work for our situation, something that can also be infrared so we can see what's happening after dark.

Georgia and I each have a night vision monocular, something we ordered early on after arriving here and setting up our hideout. While they're a lesser quality than what we would've preferred, they've worked fine so far. We've had to make choices in order to stretch our finite amount of money.

I check the rest of the driveway sensors; each seem to be lined up well and working as they should. Then I take a walk around the perimeter. Everything is fine there also.

After evaluating our alert system and assuring Georgia and the children everything looks fine, we move on with our day, starting with our private worship service. We're all thankful to have a nice, quiet Sunday.

After service, we go up the hill to listen to the radio. We thought there might be some updates on the plane crashes and bridge destruction. We're unable to get our usual station to come in. We try several others and finally find a static-riddled mess of a station out of Montana.

"What's he saying?" Georgia asks, scrunching up her face.

I shake my head, trying to listen.

"I think he said the electricity's out," Willie says, while Chloe nods.

The station fades out, and I can't get it back.

"You think the power's out around here, Dad?" Willie asks. "Maybe that's why our radio station won't come in."

"Maybe," I answer.

"It sounded like he said something about a widespread outage," Georgia says.

"You think?" I ask.

She shrugs. "Let's try it again later."

Around four o'clock, we settle in to watch a movie on the portable DVD player. Georgia picked up *E.T. the Extra-Terrestrial* yesterday—not a movie I'm particularly fond of, but Georgia loves it. I'll suffer through so the children can watch it.

We're fifteen or so minutes into the movie, and I'm nodding off when the driveway alert chimes.

"More deer?" Chloe asks.

"Not sure." I shrug. "Let's do what we need to do, and we'll find out."

Unlike yesterday, when the alert went off for the first time and caused a scare, today the children seem too casual.

"Let's go," Georgia says, spurring them to action.

Just like yesterday, I'm out the door first, heading to my perch on the shed. Georgia, the children, and Gizmo make a run for the ditch.

I've reached the shed when the second driveway alarm goes off. Unless those deer are galloping up the driveway, we have company.

I pull the radio out, click it on, and attach it to my belt. I quickly sling the carbine across my back and hoist the tactical bag over my shoulder. Climbing up the ladder with the gear and the caddy isn't easy. I've practiced it many times, but it's still a challenge. Maybe we can figure out something less clunky.

Driveway alarm number three sounds as I stretch out on the roof rungs. I don't even need the binoculars to see the pair of quads making their way up our road.

A quick look doesn't register anything out of the ordinary, just two people out for a ride. Both are dressed for riding in jeans, long-sleeved shirts, ball caps, and bandannas covering their faces. With the dirt and dust, the bandannas make sense.

Gizmo must hear them also; she sounds her own alarm. My radio goes off. "Papa Bear?"

Leaving it on my belt, I key the mic. "Company."

"Oh no," Georgia says. I hear Willie in the background trying to shush Gizmo.

"Mommy, should we run?" Chloe asks through the radio.

"Stay calm," I answer. "It's a pair of ATVs." The final driveway alert dings.

Now that we know what we're dealing with, I'll move to the second phase of our plan. I crawl down off the roof, remove the carbine, and set it within easy reach. Using the reinforced shed as cover, I'll greet the visitors from here.

Just a guy working in his shed.

I sure wish my heart wasn't pounding out of my chest. It'd make it a lot easier to be casual.

The quads slow and then shut off.

"Hello in the trailer," a strong, booming voice calls out.

"Can I help you with something?" I answer, while stepping slightly from the shed, not far out, so I can move back quickly in a hurry.

"Hi there. I'm your neighbor, Phil Hudson. This is my wife, Kelley. We've waved at each other a few times when we've been riding our quads."

He's already removed his bandanna; she slides hers down, giving me a huge smile and a slight wave.

"Yes, of course." I breathe a sigh of relief. Both are still sitting on their quads.

"Want to step off and join us for a glass of iced tea?" I ask, keying the mic so Georgia can hear.

"That'd be great, thank you."

We've only seen this couple from a distance. As he steps off his quad, I'm surprised at his size. He's slightly shorter than me but much bulkier—not fat but not super toned. He's the kind of guy that looks like a brawler, like he'd easily win a bar fight. And likely he's been in a few, judging by the slight curve of his nose.

His wife is striking, with movie star good looks. One of my early crushes was Vanessa Williams when she was Miss America. This woman is just as beautiful, with hair clipped short but stylish, and amazing eyes.

Both Phil and Kelley are around the same age as Georgia and me, maybe a few years older. The doctor in me notes he could lose a few pounds, but he isn't substantially overweight. Phil's bulk is likely a lot of muscle and limited flab. Kelley looks just about perfect.

"My wife and children are just behind the house with the dog."

"Sounds like a good watchdog," the lady, Kelley, says.

"She tries. Let me go get them."

"We're here, Sam," Georgia says, stepping around the trailer. Gizmo is pulling at the leash, shaking and shivering with excitement. Yeah, some watchdog.

I make the introductions, remembering to use the names June, Abigail, and Oliver. I don't mention our last name. Mainly because I can't remember it. Campbell? Cunningham? Something like that.

Georgia excuses herself to grab the drinks, while I escort our guests to the picnic area we've set up. The children and Gizmo go back in the house to continue their movie.

Once Georgia returns, with not only iced tea but cookies, Phil gets down to business.

"Kelley and I wanted to stop by to introduce ourselves properly and see how you folks are faring. You having any troubles?"

Georgia and I share a look. "We're fine, Phil, settling in well," I answer.

It's their turn to share a look, then Kelley quietly asks, "Do you know about the attacks?"

"Oh, yes," Georgia answers. "We don't have a television, and the radio doesn't work very well, but we've heard about both the airplanes and the bridges."

"What about the cyberattacks?" Phil asks.

Chapter 36

Georgia

"What?" Sam blurts.

I shake my head. "Cyberattacks? Like the computers are out?"

"It's not just a computer problem. The electricity is out, cell phones won't work, the internet is down, you can't use your credit cards, even traffic lights have stopped working in some areas. It started yesterday," Kelley says easily.

She has a calm, serene demeanor about her. Even so, there's a tightness around her mouth that makes me think she may not be fully cool and collected. Phil, on the other hand, does nothing to hide his concern.

"We didn't know. We tried to listen to the radio earlier, but it wouldn't come in right." I'm struggling to keep my composure.

Sam reaches over and grabs my hand, giving it a slight squeeze.

"Do you only have the solar panels?" Phil asks.

"And a generator, for now," Sam says, "until we decide on a house." He's playing our ruse well. We're relying on the hope that no one knows the estate selling this property. With it being for sale by owner and semi-neglected for some time, we pray this is the case.

"So at least you aren't affected by the power being out," Kelley says with a tight smile and a nod. "That's good."

"Yes, it is," Phil agrees. "Things might get interesting if they don't get the cyberattacks under control soon. The banks and the stock markets have already been shut down. Prospect is turning into a madhouse. It was quiet when we went into town this morning, but a fight broke out in the SuperMart. Sounded like the instigators thought they should get food for free if SuperMart couldn't take their credit card. We were fortunate to find an open gas station. Fifteen dollars a gallon, and the guy said he was getting ready to shut down. Then, when the news of the refineries came in . . . "

"What?" Sam asks.

I close my eyes. *What else?*

"Yeah, that happened today. A bunch of refineries in the Gulf and a few other places were blown up. We're in a pickle with that, for sure."

Sam squeezes my leg. I'm so glad I made another trip to town yesterday. The extra fuel and supplies I purchased will be a huge help.

"So . . . what's this mean?" I ask. "No refineries means no gas? Until when?"

"We don't know. We assume we'll have gas rations, provided they can get the power going again and fuel trucks can even deliver. We're having a meeting at the community center tonight to discuss how this affects us here in Bakerville."

"Sounds smart," Sam says.

"Yeah. It seems there was a meeting last night, too, but we didn't find out about it. So with this one, we're making sure people know. If things go bad . . . " Phil pauses, lets out a large sigh, then says, "Without power, people are going to have trouble. We're a good community here. Working together will make it easier on everyone."

Sam touches my leg again. We've been hiding out for so long, keeping to ourselves. Is it worth the risk to go to the meeting and get involved with the neighbors? I'm not sure it is.

"Are you only here for the summer?" Kelley asks.

"We're not sure," I stutter out my answer. "We were playing things by ear, but now, with these latest events . . . "

They both nod. We discuss the situation a little longer, learning much about our guests in the process. Both are retired, him from the Coast Guard and her as a psychiatric nurse.

Of course, Phil and Kelley have no idea who Sam and I really are, our medical knowledge, or his Navy experience. They think we're out-of-work chicken farmers.

The funny thing is, instead of feeling my ego crash, I find it amusing. I wonder what Sam thinks? I steal a glance at him; he looks fine, like he's very much enjoying our visit.

"So I don't know how you folks are set here as far as supplies," Phil says. "One thing we'll probably do tonight is start some plans, kick around some ideas to help people out."

Sam starts to speak, but I interrupt, not wanting him to tell these two just how much stuff we do have. "Yeah, makes sense. We're probably okay for a couple of weeks at least. Surely they'll have the cyberattack under control by then."

"We hope so." Phil gives a single nod. "We really hope so. The electricity being out is going to cause some trouble for sure, and the issue of not having cash for purchases. I guess that issue will solve itself soon enough."

"How do you mean?" Sam asks.

"Pretty soon, the stores will empty out. The power's only been out a day, and what we saw in Prospect . . . let's just say those who didn't get groceries and essential supplies this morning are probably shucks out of luck."

Sam grabs my hand, giving it a squeeze. I can almost read his mind, thanking me for being insistent about yesterday's trip to town.

I've been stocking us up on food and supplies since we moved to Bakerville. My rationale was to have things on hand in case going into town became too dangerous. Now, I'm so thankful to my paranoia—my grandiose thoughts— for providing us with necessities. We should be good for many weeks, months even.

After Phil and Kelley leave, Sam and I share a high-five, congratulating each other on pulling off our subterfuge. Then he pulls me into his arms. We spend several minutes embracing and mourning over these latest attacks. So much loss of life. And what could happen next? I take a deep breath and pull away enough to look at him.

"I think we should go to the meeting," I say.

Sam gives a shake of his head. "It's too dangerous. Maybe if Ray wouldn't have died last week. But his death put us in the headlines again."

"Maybe. But a lot has happened in the news cycle since then. And if the power and internet are out, even if someone thought they recognized us, it's not like they can Google us to confirm. We'll be fine."

"I don't know, Georgia. You told me last night how scary it was thinking the couple in the pizza joint recognized you."

"It was, Sam. Very scary. But we need to do this. If things are as bad, or could become as bad, as Phil and Kelley seem to think, we need the community. We need to be a part of a group to survive. We need— "

Sam again pulls me tight and whispers, "Neighbors. We need neighbors."

**The Mitchells' story continues in the
Havoc in Wyoming series.**

Thank you for spending your time with the Mitchells.

If you have five minutes, you'd make this writer very happy if you could write a short Amazon review. I appreciate you!

Join my reader's club!
As part of my reader's club, you'll be the first to know about new releases and specials. I also share info on books I'm reading, preparedness tips, and more.

Please sign up on my website:
MillieCopper.com

Now Available

Havoc in Wyoming

Part 1: Caldwell's Homestead

Jake and Mollie Caldwell started their small farm and homestead to be able to provide for an uncertain future for their family, friends, and community. They have tried to plan for everything. They never planned on Mollie being away on business when the terrorists attacked.

Part 2: Katie's Journey

Katie loves living on her own while finishing up her college degree, working her part-time jobs, and building a relationship with her boyfriend, Leo. When disaster strikes, being away from family isn't quite so nice, and home is over a thousand miles away. Will she make it home before the United States falls apart?

Part 3: Mollie's Quest

Two or three times a year, Mollie Caldwell travels for business. Being away from her Wyoming farmstead is both a fun time and a challenge. They started their farm to be able to provide for an uncertain future for their family, friends, and community. The farm keeps the entire family busy, meaning extra work for her husband while she's away. This time, while on her business trip, terrorists attack. Her weeklong business trip becomes much longer as she tries to make her way home.

Part 4: Shields and Ramparts

The United States, and the community of Bakerville, face a new threat . . . a threat that could change America forever. As the neighbors band together, all worry about friends and family members. Have they found safety from this latest danger?

Part 5: Fowler's Snare

Welcome to Bakerville, the sleepy Wyoming community Mollie and Jake Caldwell have chosen as their family retreat. At the edge of the wilderness, far away from the big city, they were so sure nothing bad could ever happen in such a protected place. They were wrong. Now, with the entire nation in peril, coming together as a community is the only way they can survive. But not everyone in the community has the people of Bakerville's best interest at heart.

Part 6: Pestilence in the Darkness

Surrounded by danger, they band together with the community of Bakerville to move to a new defensible location. But they weren't prepared to have to give up so much for the security they so desperately need. And they quickly learn trust must be earned, not freely given.

Part 7: My Refuge and Fortress

When Jake and a group of hunters return to Bakerville and find their former neighbors slaughtered, they realize there is a new, even more deadly threat. Will their reinforced location be secure enough? And what about the radio announcement from the president? Will his promise of help arrive in time?

Find these titles on Amazon:
www.amazon.com/author/milliecopper

Acknowledgments

Thanks to:

Ameryn Tucker my editor, proofreader, beta reader, and daughter wrapped in one. I had a story I wanted to tell, and Ameryn encouraged me and helped me bring it to life.

My husband who gave me the time and space I needed to complete this dream and was very patient as I'd tell him the same plot ideas over and over and over. Three more daughters and a young son who willingly listened to me drone on and on about story lines and ideas while encouraging me to "keep going."

Wayne Stinnett, author (WayneStinnett.com). A few years ago, I was looking for tips on moving my nonfiction PDF books to a new platform. I read Mr. Stinnett's book *Blue Collar to No Collar*, and while there were useful tips for nonfiction, what I really discovered was, I had a story I wanted to tell. As long as I can remember, I'd start creating narratives in my head and, occasionally, moving them to paper. *Blue Collar to No Collar*, and specifically Wayne's personal story, inspired me to move forward. Imagine my thrill and surprise when an email to him received a response and tips on how to proceed in my own publishing. Thank you, Mr. Stinnett! I'm also a fan of his fiction works, *Jesse McDermitt Caribbean Adventure Series* and *Charity Styles Novel Caribbean Thriller Series*—very fun reads!

My amazing Beta Readers! Tim M. for his expertise in firearms and all things that go boom, and Judy S. for always saying, "I can't wait to find out what happens next!"

And to you, my readers, for spending your time with the people of Bakerville, Wyoming. If you have five minutes, you'd make this writer very happy if you could write a short Amazon review. I appreciate you!